Earl of Basingstoke

My Sweet Scoundrels

Aileen Fish

Aspendawn Press

Contents

Contents

Chapter One

May 1815, London

Could an offer be in the near future for Lady P.W.? It could, if rumors are to be believed. A particularly scandalous earl was seen calling on her this very morning with a posy in his hands—an obvious sign of his intentions.

Lady Phoebe Woodson snapped her diary closed and set it on the small table beside her chair, patted the leather cover, then carefully aligned her inkwell to its side. She knew the dreams she wrote there were silly, but they kept her happy. Maybe one day she'd be happily married like her dear friend Marjorie, Duchess of Hartshorne. "You looked so lovely dancing with Hartshorne last night, Marjorie. Those sapphire earrings you wore matched your eyes."

"I'm exceedingly happy with him. I still have trouble believing we've been married almost seven months. To think a year ago I was ready to wed someone else." Marjorie sighed and looked toward the window, her face glowing in the sunlight streaming through the glass, which highlighted her short, black curls.

"You two are perfect for each other. Now it's my turn. I must find the man who's perfect for me. I'm twenty-four and am still single, isn't it shocking? Papa has been giving me stern looks when each day passes without a gentleman sending flowers or asking to walk with me at Hyde Park. This year, I vow to not return to the country without accepting a proposal."

In truth, Phoebe had already found the man she desired with all her heart. She'd brushed aside flirtations from three men over the years, unable to consider anyone but him—Nathan Carruthers, Earl of Basingstoke. With his wickedly handsome features and glittering brown eyes, he was the most desirable man of her acquaintance.

At least, she assumed his eyes were brown, and they must glitter, given how his smile brightened his face. She'd never stood close enough to be certain of the shade. Never danced with him, nor pretended to stumble so she could fall into his arms.

A deep sigh escaped as her shoulders slumped.

Her problem was getting Basingstoke to notice her. They'd been introduced three years ago, but for all she knew, he'd promptly forgotten her.

"Do you think he'll attend Lady Albright's ball tonight?" Phoebe asked.

"Who? Hart won't be there. He mentioned meeting a friend at his club."

"Silly me—I forget you cannot hear what I think." The friends laughed. "We've known each other so long I sometimes believe I know exactly what you're thinking."

"Ah, now I understand," Marjorie said. "You meant Basingstoke."

Phoebe actually blushed like a silly debutante, her cheeks burning so much they must be bright red. "I'm foolish to think of him, aren't I?"

"You're foolish to think your father would allow you to even dance with him, much less marry. Those friends of his...the scandals...the rumors...even if only half are true, those men are truly wicked."

"But doesn't the thought of kissing one of those scoundrels excite you, just a little?" Seeing Marjorie's frown, Phoebe reconsidered. "Well, wouldn't it have before you married? The gossip surrounding them might be as exaggerated as your husband's situation was. Hartshorne wasn't guilty of that scandal with his brother's wife. Or rather, with the woman his brother ended up marrying. That would have been quite the scandal the other way, wouldn't it?"

Marjorie's scowl hadn't softened. "That *W* pin on Basingstoke's lapel tells you all you need to know about him. Wicked. Your parents would never forgive you for associating with such a man, and you'd be ruined in Society's eyes."

"Very well, I'll forget about Basingstoke." She knew very well she lied as she spoke the words. She'd never forget the earl, though she could refrain from speaking about him. However, she wouldn't stop detailing the rumors surrounding him in her diary. Embellishing them...making herself the willing victim of his debauchery, or what she assumed that entailed. Those stories she wrote might be as close as she ever came to a grand romance, so she'd take her enjoyment where she could find it.

Nathan Carruthers, Earl of Basingstoke, scooped his winnings from the center of the table and stacked the coins in neat columns with his prior winnings. The club he and the so-called Wicked Earls frequented was quiet, the smell of stale pipe smoke lingering in the air. His friends and fellow earls, Grayson and Weston, passed their cards to the dealer, Sussex.

Grayson drank from his glass. "What's this rumor I hear about you, Basingstoke? You're planning to leave the club soon?"

"Leave? Never!" He eyed each of his friends, searching for the laughter they must be holding back.

"That's not what I heard. You've decided to end your days of freedom and marry." Sussex shuffled the cards and dealt.

Basingstoke coughed to cover his gasp of surprise. He'd mentioned something of the sort to his friend, the Duke of Thornton, but Thorn was very tight-lipped. Who could have overheard? "That's not precisely what I said. I don't think I mentioned marriage, as such. I simply said it might be time to consider a family."

The three men laughed loudly, and Basingstoke gritted his teeth, glancing around the room to see who looked their way at the outburst.

"Last I heard, the one required the other, at least for a man of our station," Weston said. "Although, the *ton* is convinced you've already fathered a son."

"Leave Benjamin out of this discussion, or any other!" Basingstoke scowled at his friend.

Grayson nodded. "Back to marriage...what could have put such a thought into your head? You're young...what, eight-and-twenty?"

"I'm twenty-nine, but that's beside the point." Nothing had caused him to awaken one day and decide he needed a wife. Several members of their club had lately found love, but he wasn't envious of them.

He didn't think so, anyway. No, this idea was a whisper that he heard at odd moments of the day while riding his horse, or sitting alone with a book. A very subtle notion that he should probably ignore.

But he was beginning to like the idea. Not the part where he had to search for the right young lady—he dreaded that the most. The result...the feeling of satisfaction when he sat opposite his wife at breakfast, or read aloud to her in the evening under the glow of a lamp, those moments were what he looked forward to.

In other words, a marriage completely unlike his parents'.

"Basingstoke, when you're done wool-gathering, it's your call."

He wasn't even certain which one of the men spoke, but he quickly took his turn before anyone else could add to the good-natured derision.

In the morning, he would finally look at the invitations piled on his desk and see where to begin his search. He had no fear of running into one of the wicked earls in a ballroom, so he could enjoy his evening without the catcalls they'd likely offer.

Chapter Two

A certain notoriously wicked earl is rumored to have fallen madly and quite passionately in love with the diamond Lady P.W. Our sources are uncertain if the feelings are returned. Is there heartbreak in store for the Earl of B~?

The next evening, Basingstoke stood shoulder-to-shoulder with the other finely dressed members of society who waited to enter Almack's. He'd presumed he was less likely to be turned away at this door than at any ballroom, even if he had an invitation. Some of those matrons invited the most scandalous men they could, just to be able to say, "Do you know who refused my invitation?" Then they'd expound on what sort of debauchery kept him from coming.

Lady Sefton, one of the patronesses of Almack's Assembly Rooms, was an old friend of his mother's and she was likely the one who insisted he be granted permission to purchase a voucher each year, although he rarely used it. This Season, he would use the ten-guinea cost of the annual subscription to its utmost.

Even if it killed him.

Skirting the red velvet ropes marking the dance floor, he searched for somewhere to begin the undesirable task of socializing. He had no idea which young ladies were par-

ticipating in the foolishness known as the marriage mart, and which ones intended to lead her suitors along like puppies, only to refuse a proposal. If one of his friends was in attendance, he could ask, but that was unlikely as his friends avoided these events at all costs.

From the corner of his eye, he noticed Thornton disappearing into the card room. Thorn would be a good person to ask, since those looking for marriage were exactly the sort of lady he avoided.

Now that he thought about it, joining a card game would allow Basingstoke to catch up on the gossip involving someone other than himself, for a change.

He abhorred gossip, but at times like this, it was his best tool.

The table where Thorn sat had four other men already seated there, but Basingstoke pulled a chair from along the wall and muscled his way between two of the players.

"You won't find a wife in here," Thorn said with a sly grin as he placed his bet.

"I'm hoping you men can save me some time. To which young ladies should I request an introduction?"

One of the men chuckled and shook his head. "Why do you think we're in here? To avoid conversing and dancing with the ladies. How on earth could we be expected to know who's in the other room, aside from our wives and sisters?"

The other men laughed in agreement.

The older brother of one of this Season's diamonds eyed Basingstoke, grimaced, and sighed. "What sort of girl are you looking for? I'm assuming you understand my sister isn't for you."

"Of course." What did he want? He hadn't thought much about it, assuming he'd know it when he saw it. Or met her. "Well, she must be pretty—"

The men laughed again and derided him for insisting appearance mattered.

"I am in earnest. A pretty wife will have pretty daughters, which will make it much easier for them to marry. I'm considering their needs, not my own."

"You've got this well planned," Thorn said, "for someone who's just decided to marry."

"As well I should. I'll share my home with this woman for the rest of my life, and she'll be the mother of my children. How can I know if she suits, if I don't know what I want?"

He kept the other qualities to himself. She must be an avid reader, or at the very least be willing to listen to him read to her. That made him sound like a popinjay, to be sure, but it was important. He didn't care what her income was, as long as she wasn't extravagant. Wanting her to come from a scandal-free family wasn't something he held out hope for, given his reputation—and his father's lifestyle.

Maybe he should wait another year to marry. He shouldn't rush a decision like this. Just because his friends lately found love and happiness didn't mean the commodity was going to dry up soon.

The urge to join these men at the table and forget all other foolishness hit strong, but he could play cards in his club at any time. Still... "Deal me in."

Three of the men, including Thorn, stopped what they were doing and turned toward him.

He shrugged. "Can't I play a few hands before dancing?"

They all stared, and Thorn cleared his throat.

"You'd think you all were my father," Basingstoke said. "I'm a grown man, I can make my own decisions."

"Of course, you can," Thorn said. "And we can decide not to let you play."

"What do any of you have to gain by my marrying?"

"Nothing at all," the dealer, a gray-haired older man, said. "But if you play, we stand to lose plenty. Be off with you, lad, and let us continue."

Feeling fully chastised, Basingstoke shook his head and shoved back his seat. In a move of pettiness, he didn't bother to return the chair to the spot where he'd found it. He was certain everyone in the room had just witnessed his dismissal. He'd never been treated that way, and it took every ounce of his nerve not to protest and demand the respect he was due.

Yet Thorn was right. He hadn't come here to play cards.

Finding a bride was hard work, he was sure of it, and he might as well get this whole ordeal behind him.

Returning to the ballroom, he again skirted the velvet ropes, this time in search of Lady Sefton, who would leap at the chance to show off one of her favorite scoundrels. Several young ladies—very young, by the look of them, not to his tastes at all—fluttered their eyelashes or fans while watching him pass, only to be nudged by a chaperone so they snapped their gazes away.

This behavior would make this business much easier, narrowing the list of women to consider. Her parents must approve of the betrothal, and he wasn't going to beg for acceptance. Showing their distaste for him before an introduction was made allowed him to simply walk on by.

To his surprise, a pretty lady with brown hair twisted into an elaborate knot on the back of her head, and bright, sparkling eyes, smiled when he looked her way. Her manner was different to the others, more glad than flirtatious, which intrigued him. He didn't recognize her, nor did he see anyone nearby whom he could ask for an introduction. He'd have to wait until he found Lady Sefton.

That person was on the far side of the room, and by the time he reached her, there was no sign of the smiling young lady.

"Lord Basingstoke, I'm pleased to see you've decided to make use of your voucher. I've wondered when that time would come." Lady Sefton took his arm and joined him on his path around the dancers.

"You can't convince me my presence has been missed."

"By the matrons, no. However, I've become bored with the lack of a good scandal. Please indulge me." The rolled fabric of her turban forced her to lean away to look up at him as she talked. She spoke good-naturedly, with an undeniable twinkle in her eye.

"I'm afraid I must disappoint you. I'm hoping to put those in my past."

"I see, and that's why you're here. I can scarcely believe that day has arrived. Since you've sought me out, you must wish for an introduction. Any particular lady, or shall I choose one I think you'd find desirable?"

"I saw a brown-haired girl who seemed to know me, but I didn't recognize her. Shall we begin there?"

"Only if you give me more details than hair color."

"Lavender gown with sort of..." he tried to demonstrate the fit of her sleeves, then waved his arms down his front and outward to indicate her hem, "and flowers. Here, and there."

Shaking her head, she smiled. "You are hopelessly male. That description hardly helps, but in the meantime, I will be the envy of the matrons with such a handsome young man at my side. Come, show me your young lady."

She wasn't flirting. It was an honest statement demonstrated by the looks they garnered.

An older woman with full curves packed into a tight, straight gown, and an ostrich feather rising above her turban, rushed to block their path. "Lady Sefton, you look lovely this evening."

"Lady Lucas, how delightful." Lady Sefton's voice bordered on sarcasm.

The matron fluttered her hand at her two daughters. "Girls, come here." She smiled again at Basingstoke.

Lady Sefton caught his eye. "Lord Basingstoke, this is Lady Lucas, wife of Sir Harrison Lucas, and their daughters, Miss Lucas and Miss Elaina."

He dipped his head in acknowledgment, hoping they'd move away now that the matron had gained her introduction. He was not that lucky.

"My lord, my eldest daughter has the next set open. There are so few gentlemen here tonight. It's difficult for all the young ladies to find partners."

The poor girl in question turned a delicate shade of pink, stirring Basingstoke's pity.

"How lucky for me," he said, tipping his head and smiling politely as he spoke through gritted teeth. "I find myself without a partner also."

Two entire dance sets passed by the time he'd escorted her sister, too, and he was once again free to search for the lovely vision in lavender and gain an introduction. While approaching Lady Sefton, he saw the beauty among the dancers. Catching the matron's attention, he tipped his head toward the crowded floor and mouthed, "There, that's the one."

Peering through her lorgnette as Basingstoke reached her, Lady Sefton nodded. "Ah, yes. Excellent taste, my lord. She is Lady Phoebe Woodson, daughter of the Earl of Appledown. Come, we'll find Lady Appledown and make you known to her."

The woman at his side didn't dally, but marched straight toward a tallish woman in deep red, her pace hurried as if she had the most interesting *on-dit* to share. That much was true—he wanted to meet Lady Phoebe, which would give Lady Appledown something to talk about for weeks, whether she was pleased with him or not.

"My dear friend," Lady Sefton began, "have you met Lord Basingstoke? His mother and I have been friends...well, longer than either of us will own to."

The matron studied him, her expression unreadable. "I don't believe I have. Good evening, sir."

"What do you think of the number of attendees tonight?" he asked, aiming for a neutral conversation until he could guess her opinion of him. "Is it always so crowded?"

Their small talk continued until the music ended. Basingstoke stole a covert glance to see if Lady Phoebe approached from the dance floor. She'd been on the far side of the room, so the wait for her to join them seemed unending.

"Lady Phoebe," Lady Sefton said when the girl arrived, "I am delighted to introduce you to Lord Basingstoke."

She curtsied. "In truth, we've already met, but it was

several years ago. I was with the Duke of Hartshorne and Lady Marjorie, as she was then. They've married now, as I'm sure you know."

What a cad he was not to remember her. How was it possible not to have noticed her? It must have happened after one of the three-day card games at the club, when he wasn't even sure of his own name. "I'm chagrined to realize I don't recall our meeting. May I make it up to you? I'd be honored if you'd dance with me."

Phoebe fought not to gape at the earl. Basingstoke was here, in front of her—in front of half of Polite Society—asking her to dance. Was this truly happening, or was she home in her bed, asleep? "I'd enjoy that, sir."

She didn't even check to see what her mother said, but quickly walked with him toward the musicians, who were preparing for the next set. Her heart pounded hard enough that he must have been able to hear it, and her hands shook with excitement. Holding his arm was an awkward exercise between squeezing hard enough to still her hands or allowing his blood to reach his fingers.

"I don't believe I've seen you at an assembly this Season, my lord."

"I haven't been to any."

"Well, we're honored that you've chosen to break that habit." Oh, that was horrid! She sounded like she was being sarcastic. She had to say something nice. Something to make him glad he asked her to dance. Something flirtatious. "I'll be the envy of everyone."

She looked away so she couldn't see if he was regretting his choice of partner already.

He said nothing.

They lined up with the other dancers and awaited the music. Lord Basingstoke's gaze was steady on her, as though he was reading her. What did he see? Did he judge her favorably? When the steps allowed them to approach each other, she asked, "Are you in Town long?"

"I spend most of my time here."

She knew that fact from gossip. She also knew he frequented a private gentlemen's club with other men of scandal, a place known as The Wicked Earls' Club, and that he often called on a certain "boarding" house for young women, neither of which she cared about. It made him all the more exciting.

Of course, the boarding house visits would have to cease upon their betrothal.

"Do you plan to be more social before everyone returns to the country?" She choked on her wording. "That is, may we expect to see you at other assemblies, now that you've seen we aren't too horribly dull?"

He had to wait until the dance brought them together again to speak, but he watched her the entire time, a sly grin softening the hard lines of his face. "Dull would be the last word I'd use to describe you."

Her heart fluttered, and a wave of heat rose up her neck. "I'm not certain how to take that."

"I mean the words as a complement, to be sure. You intrigue me."

She lowered her gaze. Such a relief. He didn't find her dull. It was a start.

Their set of dances left her warm and tired, from all the bouncing steps combined with her excitement. Basingstoke must have noticed. "Shall we get some lemonade?"

We. He wanted her to go with him, not return to her mother and wait for him to fetch a glass. Such a trivial thing to become excited over, but she didn't care.

"Yes, thank you."

He offered his arm, and she took it gladly, holding her head high as they crossed to the refreshment room. Oh, the stares and glares she received! This one moment was the highlight of the Season—so far, at least.

Her dear friend, Lady Clara Swinton, must have gasped,

for her mouth formed a perfect *O*, and her eyes were almost as wide as her mouth. Phoebe made a mental note to walk to the park with Clara in the morning and tell her every word the earl spoke.

"Here's an empty chair," he said. "Why don't you sit, and I'll get our drinks."

She did, then tried to look nonchalant, as if being in the company of a scoundrel was nothing out of the ordinary for her.

When he approached a few minutes later, his gaze pinned her in place, but his expression was unreadable. He smiled, but she didn't know him well enough to know if it reflected pleasure or was merely polite.

Reaching for the glass he offered, she thanked him and took a sip. Before she could swallow, her mother bustled through the doorway with Lady Sefton in her wake. Mama marched to the center of the room, clearly searching for Phoebe, whose face grew scalding hot in mortification. She choked on her lemonade.

Clearing her throat, she rose. "My mother must be looking for me."

When he turned, Basingstoke couldn't have missed her mother's glare upon spotting them. He reached for Phoebe's glass. "I imagine she'll want you to return to the dancers. In my quest to know you better, I didn't consider the other gentlemen who wish to partner with you."

He must know other gentlemen were the last thing on her mother's mind. Phoebe gave him an apologetic smile. "I should have thought to tell her where we were going."

Mama pushed through the crowd and stopped abruptly in front of them. "There you are, daughter! Come, it's time we went home."

"But Mama—"

"My feet are tired, and I fear a headache is coming on." She didn't acknowledge Basingstoke's presence.

Lady Sefton joined their tense little party. "My lord and ladies, isn't the music most pleasant this evening?"

Mama remained silent.

Basingstoke glared at Mama.

"Why yes," Phoebe said. "The quartet has a new violinist, I believe."

Exhaling in a huff, Mama nodded. "They're very good."

"Lord Basingstoke," Lady Sefton continued, "you and Lady Phoebe were a delight to watch."

People were watching at that very moment, leaning closer to overhear exactly what was being said. Phoebe prayed nothing would be worth repeating.

Basingstoke bowed his head. "She is such a graceful dancer, she makes even my uncoordinated steps look good."

"You're too modest, sir," Phoebe said quickly.

Mama's lips were pinched in a tight, thin line, a sure sign she was working hard to refrain from speaking.

Lady Sefton continued her rescue of the uncomfortable situation. "My lord, there's someone who wishes to make your acquaintance. Ladies, will you allow me to steal this charming, handsome young man away?"

"Of course," Phoebe said quickly. "We cannot presume to spoil the evening for all the other young ladies hoping for a chance to dance with the earl."

Basingstoke merely lifted an eyebrow as he studied her intently. Then he took his bow. "Lady Phoebe, I look forward to the next time we meet."

He wanted to see her again. Phoebe's mouth went dry, and she sighed. He was a dream.

Her dream was coming to life.

As he walked away, Mama harrumphed beside her. "'The next time we meet.' The nerve of the man. As if I'll allow you to be seen with him again. Why, I fully intended to refuse his offer of a dance with you, but you walked away before I could. You mustn't do that again."

"Mama, we danced and sought refreshment fully in the eyes of everyone. No scandal took place. No one will make note of our dance, beyond the fact he was here and dancing, of course. I wasn't the first one he asked, so it meant nothing."

Oh, please don't let it mean nothing.

How would she ever decide which assembly invitations to accept in the weeks ahead to better her chances of seeing him again? She, Marjorie, and Clara must discuss this first thing in the morning. Since she'd never be able to fall asleep, the hours in bed would give her plenty of time to make a list of places to go this Season.

This couldn't be the only time she'd speak with him. Life couldn't be so cruel. She vowed to do everything she could to make certain she saw him as often as possible.

Chapter Three

Last night at Almack's, a particular earl was observed dancing with a certain Lady P.W . three times! A short time later, it was remarked upon that neither person could be found. Lady P.W. was later discovered beside her friend, the Duchess of H. Where had she been hiding, and who had she been hiding with?

The following morning, Phoebe's joy knew no bounds when a posy of violets arrived with a note from Basingstoke saying that he would call that afternoon to walk with Phoebe.

Mama, eating breakfast across the table from Phoebe, was not pleased. "That man! Of all the gentlemen you've met, why him?"

"I don't know, Mama. When I look upon him my stomach shivers. If he turns my way, and if he smiles, I feel as though I might swoon."

"Hmph. Neither of those will make for a happy life. I'll admit his income is better than many, and his family seat is one of the finer homes in all of England. But his reputation, his character... You know your father won't allow the match."

"Why? What has he done that most men haven't? Prinny, himself—"

With narrowed eyelids, Mama glared. "Your father is not a favorite of the Prince Regent, so he wouldn't approve of your marrying the Prince, either."

"Won't you try to know Basingstoke better before refusing his calls? Or let me know him. I might realize he's not the man for me, after all."

"I highly doubt that. I've seen how you look at him. You're deeply infatuated with him already, and nothing beyond marriage will allow you to see the truth. He's a charming man, and I use the term as in a snake charmer. He'll only show you the qualities you desire. Then when you're married and have provided him with an heir, he'll return to his wild ways."

"Men mature at some point, don't they? Most give up their wild ways upon marrying." At least, that's what Phoebe hoped. None of her friends complained of their husbands' behavior. None of them had been accused of any sort of scandal she was aware of, but surely, they'd had some bad habits they gave up.

Life was too unfair. All she wanted was to be loved by the Earl of Basingstoke. Now that she had her chance, her parents were going to thwart it.

Patting her lips with her white linen serviette, Phoebe pushed her plate aside and drank some tea. Try as she might, she couldn't get her cold toast past the lump in her throat. "Mama, you can't embarrass me by refusing his call. People will assume he refused me, not the other way around. Some will say I was saved by it, but many will deem it proof I'm not a desirable match. Can't we find a way to let this end naturally? I can tell him there's someone else."

"How is that different from simply refusing his call today?" Mama argued while daintily slicing a sausage.

It wasn't different, but Phoebe would never admit it. Instead, she excused herself and went to her room to write to her friends and beg their assistance.

The notes she sent Marjorie and Clara were identical except for the salutation.

Basingstoke will call on me today! Mama wants to refuse him, but I must see him, I must! If it wouldn't be so horribly inappropriate, I'd await him on the street, just so he couldn't be turned away. I will *find a way to see him. I'll let you know what transpires at the soonest possible moment.*

If, somehow, Mama succeeds in keeping me from seeing him, I beg you both will help me find a way.

Yrs. Phoebe

Basingstoke strode up the front steps at the home of the Earl and Countess of Appledown and realized for the first time in memory he was apprehensive about how he'd be received. The way the countess had behaved when he and Lady Phoebe sought refreshments at Almack's, he doubted she'd be pleased to see him. He wouldn't be surprised to be informed the family wasn't at home.

Instead, the regal-looking butler in gold livery stepped aside to allow him in. "The ladies are in the front drawing room. This way, please."

The large entry suited the butler's uniform, with Italian marble-topped tables lining the walls and gilt-framed landscapes hanging between gold sconces. The overall effect was much too ostentatious for Basingstoke's taste.

"Lord Basingstoke," the butler announced as the earl passed through the open doors.

Lady Appledown stood slowly, her face a polite mask. "My lord, how good of you to call. Will you sit?"

Standing in front of the window, Lady Phoebe was lit from behind, the sunlight surrounding her in a halo of brightness. Her smile was even brighter. Moving out of the light, she gracefully perched on the edge of a chair. "Lord Basingstoke, I'm pleased to see you."

He chose to ignore her mother's obvious displeasure and took a seat.

"I received your flowers this morning, they're very pretty," Lady Phoebe said.

"Their beauty doesn't compare to yours," he replied.

Showing her disapproval, Lady Appledown sniffed loudly.

He again chose to ignore her. "You were by far the fairest of the young ladies at Almack's. I noticed how many of the men were jealous of my dancing with you."

His little beauty rolled her hazel eyes. "Really, my lord, you do exaggerate. The others had an equal opportunity to partner with me, but they didn't ask."

The smile on those lovely lips was more coy than happy, a fact he found most intriguing. Despite her mother's stern scowl, the young lady flirted with him. It was a complete reversal of the first glance they'd exchanged last night.

"There's a warmish breeze this afternoon. With your mother's permission, I'd enjoy walking with you." He glanced at the countess and was met by that piercing glare.

Pursing her lips tightly, the countess gave a sharp nod.

Nearly jumping to her feet, Lady Phoebe said, "Let me fetch my bonnet and my maid to chaperone us."

Once they reached the street, they strolled side-by-side. When Basingstoke paused to let her pass ahead of him around a nanny with a group of children, Lady Phoebe's delicate rosewater scent teased his senses. "Your mother doesn't approve of me," he said when he was beside her again.

She lowered her gaze as though something on the street fascinated her. "Is that uncommon? No disrespect, my lord, but that *W* pin you wear isn't intended to impress the mothers of marriageable daughters."

"You're very direct. I enjoy that. It's a refreshing change."

"My mother doesn't think so. She cringes when she hears me. I'm not the daughter she hoped for." Lady Phoebe peered from behind the brim of her bonnet. "I can't conform. Oh, I'll keep my peace when needed, even if I must bite my tongue to do so, but..."

Now she ducked her head. "I believe this is one of

those times I should remain silent. Forgive me, Lord Basingstoke."

"Promise me you'll never hold back when you speak to me." He fought a sudden need to reach for her hand. The gossips would have enough to talk about without him taking liberties.

What was happening to him? He was totally besotted over a lady he'd met only the night before. If he could secure her affection as easily as his had claimed her, this whole marriage nonsense could be resolved quickly.

Basingstoke continued to watch her as they strolled, memorizing the lines of her profile. A delicate chin, a pert little nose, topped by an unlined brow. "Do you enjoy the opera?"

"Of course."

"Is that your true opinion, or what all young ladies are expected to say?"

She laughed, taunting him again with that coy smile. "We had this discussion only moments ago. I'll always be honest with you."

"I'm pleased to hear it. Will you accompany me to the opera tomorrow evening?"

"I'd like that, thank you."

They continued on for several blocks before turning back, neither speaking. It was as though nothing more needed to be said. The quiet between them wasn't strained, but rather filled with contentment and a peculiar sort of peace.

Basingstoke rather liked this new feeling of being so comfortable in the company of a woman. How soon could he ask her father's permission to marry, without seeming desperate?

Desperation be damned, he—like Lady Phoebe—refused to conform to the constraints of Polite Society. He would propose as soon as he saw fit to do so.

Chapter Four

Could Lord B~ have finally recognized his own heart?

After leaving Lady Phoebe, Basingstoke returned home where his secretary, Phil Ingraham, was busy writing at the smaller of the two desks in his office. "Do you have the file on the children?" Basingstoke asked, coming to stand at the man's elbow.

Ingraham glanced up and pushed his spectacles up his nose. "It's on your desk blotter." Running his left hand through the hair flopping over his forehead, he returned to his scribbles.

"Thank you."

Ridgewell, his butler, paused inside the doorway. "Would you like your coffee brought now?"

"Please. That will be all." Basingstoke rearranged the objects on his desktop before opening the folder in the center of the stacks of paper and books. He took out the list of names and set it to one side, then scanned the other pages. He set aside Benjamin's sheet, as that investigation was closed. He should create a new folder for the completed investigations, and perhaps one for the dead ends, although he didn't like to think of any line of inquiry as being completely dead. As long as some of the witnesses were living, they might suddenly recall a bit of gossip that would give Basingstoke new avenues to pursue.

He'd made this his life's mission, and he wouldn't stop working until every child had been identified and located.

This was the only way he'd been able to assuage any of the guilt he carried in being his father's son, and some nights when he lay awake he didn't think he'd live long enough to make amends for everything his father had done.

Their evening at the opera went so well, Basingstoke invited Lady Phoebe to the Egyptian Hall the next afternoon to see the new items added to the exhibit from the Americas. The Duke of Hartshorne and his wife chaperoned them, and their relaxed supervision gave them the freedom to speak alone, albeit in a crowd of strangers.

With the weather being so nice, they walked several blocks to the museum. He continually studied her from the corner of his eye, taking in her small, rosy mouth and the curve of her neck. Her pale skin glowed with healthy beauty.

And if he wasn't careful, he'd fall at her feet and beg for one more glimpse of her sweet smile.

Yet she always smiled...an honest smile from within, at least when she looked at him.

Stop, man! Lady Phoebe wasn't the sort to allow puppies to lap at her heels, and he must prove he's the sort of man she wants to marry. He grunted in disgust. "Prove myself."

"I beg your pardon?"

Had he spoken out loud? He grimaced. "I—I hope to prove to myself that I remember my studies when I see the exhibits."

She shaded her eyes and studied him. "Do you enjoy history?"

"I don't spend a lot of time thinking about it, so I suppose not."

"Then it's a good thing I do, or our afternoon would be quite dull."

"Dull, you say?" He rose to the challenge. "My company is never dull."

To prove his statement, he trotted across the street and bought a rose from a flower girl. Breaking the stem to a short length, he tucked it among the silk flowers on Lady Phoebe's bonnet. The red clashed horribly with the peach blooms, defeating his entire purpose. Removing it, he said, "Alas, this bud is ashamed of how poorly it looks next to your beauty."

When he lifted his arm to toss it into the street, Lady Phoebe grasped his sleeve. "Don't you dare throw it away."

He studied the bud in his hand. "That would be a sorry thing to do, wouldn't it."

She held out her palm. He set the flower in it. She lifted it to her nose and inhaled. The smile spreading on her lips was angelic.

It hit him like a horse kicking his gut. He sucked in air so he could speak. "The rose is pleased to have brought you joy."

"You know what a flower is thinking?"

"Why do they exist but to bring joy to all who look upon them?" What was he doing? Next, he'd begin spouting poetry. Basingstoke was relieved his friends weren't there to hear him. They'd ban him from the Wicked Earls' Club long before he married, which was the only reason any of them left.

"You're right, you aren't dull, but I never imagined you would be."

"Do you spend many hours each day contemplating my charm?"

Her cheeks reddened. He'd struck a nerve. Did she think of him as often as he did her? "That many hours? I see. And am I equal to what you've imagined?"

The emotion in her eyes nearly overwhelmed him. Happiness—or was it delight? How would one differ to the other? Some sort of affection was there, unless he was wishful thinking.

He preferred to believe it was there.

Looking ahead, he realized they'd reached the Egyptian Hall. He paused and waited for the duke and duchess to join them before entering.

"Lady Phoebe," Hartshorne said as he held the door open for the ladies, "your cheeks have a bit of color. Perhaps we were too long in the sun. I'll have my carriage brought around for our trip home."

"Thank you," she said, ducking her head as she removed her bonnet.

Basingstoke said nothing, knowing their flirting had more to do with her blush than the sun. They got on so well together. That boded well for a happy future.

Once his eyes adjusted to the interior light, he scanned the room. "Where do we begin? On the left, then make our way around?"

"That makes as much sense as any plan." Lady Phoebe began to walk in that direction.

He forced himself to don a sober façade, not aloof but as far from lovesick fool as possible. With Hartshorne and the duchess walking with them, his temptation to flirt was tempered. Just a bit.

The first display contained items collected from the Americas, an assortment of pottery and gold items. Marjorie—Her Grace—studied the pottery, saying, "These vessels are interesting. Some are so primitive, and some are so detailed as to compare to Greek statues."

She was correct. The ones that could have been crafted by a child had exaggerated features, and red markings in the form of tattoos or garment embellishments.

"That one has giraffe spots," Hartshorne commented.

"I doubt they'd seen giraffes so long ago, when they only had small boats to travel in." Lady Phoebe looked to Basingstoke as if for confirmation.

"Excellent point," he responded.

Their discussion continued as they circled the room,

making casual remarks about the curious findings on display. He was enjoying the time almost disproportionately. Just being with Lady Phoebe made the time pass much too quickly.

Then the spiteful gossips noticed them.

"It's not surprising she is with a man of his character," said one man. "Just look at her friend. Lady Marjorie, as she was then, married the Duke of Hartshorne despite him disgracing that girl. You know, the one the brother stepped up and married. Now *there* was a good man."

Basingstoke bristled, glancing askance at Hartshorne to see if he'd heard. If he had, he was doing an excellent job of keeping his features schooled.

A woman with that man added her point of view. "One would imagine Lady Phoebe's parents would have forbidden her from associating with the couple. It's a shame such a sweet girl should fall into the hands of that man, Basingstoke."

The duchess walked up to stand beside Lady Phoebe. She pointed to a gold figure. "Do you suppose the half-circle headdress he wears represents the sun or the moon?"

"My initial thought," said Hartshorne, "Was that it was feathers, but I see no feather demarcation, so it must be one or the other as you say."

The gossips weren't finished. "What do you imagine Lady Phoebe thinks of the by-blow? She must know of the boy. How can she allow herself to be seen in public with Basingstoke?"

"Such a shame to see the ruin of two such respectable families," the man said.

Basingstoke had heard enough. He tucked Lady Phoebe's hand to his side and led his party to another display. His vision burned red, and his body shook with the restraint it took not to react. Nothing he said to the rumormongers would stop them from spreading their vicious, incorrect tales. All he could do was try to shield Lady Phoebe from hearing them. At some point the gossips would find something new to focus upon, and he and

Lady Phoebe could enjoy their lives together.

"Let's continue to the next exhibit. I think we've seen everything there is to see here." Without waiting for a response, Basingstoke strode to the next room. There, realizing he'd practically dragged Lady Phoebe along, he slowed, and paused in front of a collection of Greek artifacts.

But the gossip continued. "Do you suppose he's compromised her already? How long do you think it will be before he moves on to his next victim?"

Enough.

Basingstoke marched to the offending couple, neither of whom he recognized. "You seem to have quite a fascination with my life, and that of my friends. Yet you are incorrect in many of the crimes we supposedly committed against society. I suggest you stop talking about us, or the Duke of Hartshorne will speak to the proprietor about having you removed from the premises."

That said, he returned to his friends.

"Hear, hear," Hartshorne said loudly enough for no one to miss.

"Thank you," added the duchess.

Lady Phoebe's gaze held a hint of something new—respect, or pride, perhaps? "Yes, thank you for coming to my rescue."

"I will always do my best to shield you from harm, physical or verbal." Basingstoke reached for her hand and held it to his chest. "Your happiness is important to me."

Her answering smile was shy, and she ducked her head. Lifting the rose to her nose, she inhaled.

A slight portion of the weight he carried on his conscience lifted. He mightn't be capable of keeping Lady Phoebe from overhearing those hurtful words, but he could make it clear how much he wanted to protect her from being wounded by them.

That was all he could do.

Chapter Five

That wicked Lord B~ has been seen once again with Lady P.W. They are becoming quite the couple. Could there be a betrothal in the offing?

Giggling, Phoebe closed her journal and leaned back in her seat to look out the window. She was foolish to think Basingstoke would fall in love with her—at least, in a matter of mere days. Yet what else could she think? In the weeks since they'd been re-introduced at Almack's, he'd called on her at home multiple times, taken her to the opera once, and last night they danced both the supper dance and the final set of the evening. He'd escorted her and her mother to their carriage and promised to call soon.

He must be in love. There was no other explanation. No explanation she wished to hear, perhaps.

When a footman announced Marjorie was waiting for her in the morning room, Phoebe hurried downstairs. Rushing across the red wool carpet, she grasped Marjorie's hands. "I'm so happy!"

Marjorie shook her head, chuckling. "If he'd done something like kissing you or proposing, you'd have called upon me first thing this morning. What has you so cheerful?"

"Life. Love. Lord Basingstoke." She sighed, drawing the breath from all the way down in her toes. "They're all the same thing."

"You might think differently when you read this." Marjorie handed her the morning newspaper. "Mrs. Crookshank's column."

"I've caught Mrs. Crookshank's eye? What does she say?" Phoebe snatched the paper.

"You won't be so pleased when you read it. Neither will your parents."

Skimming down the column, Phoebe came to the paragraph in question. She read aloud. "Lady P.W. was seen entering a carriage several hours after leaving Lady D~'s ball. The fact the carriage was parked in front of Lord B~'s town house couldn't mean what it appears to do. Could it?"

Phoebe lowered the newspaper and met Marjorie's gaze, imploring, "Tell me this isn't true."

"You're the one who would know that, not me."

"I mean, tell me this isn't really in the paper. They're accusing me of having a liaison with Basingstoke. This is a joke, isn't it?"

Leading her to the nearest chair, Marjorie said, "You just read it. Tell me you didn't..."

"Didn't what?" Phoebe tensed with shock and anger. "How could you even consider the idea? I thought you were my friend."

"I am. I'm sorry. Who do you suppose it was seen at his home?"

"Who says anyone was there? Mrs. Crookshank creates most of the gossip based on her own whims. The true problem is that others will believe it. Mama will never let me leave the house again."

"You have more to worry about than that. No other man will have you as his wife, now. Not after someone claims to have seen you leaving the earl's house alone in the middle of the night."

Tossing the newspaper onto the table beside her, Phoebe rose and began to pace, pinching her index finger with her other hand to allow herself to focus. "Basingstoke is the only man whose opinion concerns me, and he'll know the truth of it."

"Your father will never allow you to marry the earl. I'm truly amazed your mother continues to let you be seen with him. That will come to an end now. She'll likely take you back to the country."

Father never read those columns, but someone would show it to him at some point during the day, she was sure. Then she'd have to face his displeasure.

Phoebe didn't have to wait more than a few minutes before Father slammed the front door behind him as he entered, bellowing, "Bring my daughter to me!"

Meeting Marjorie's gaze, Phoebe chewed her lower lip. "Will you wait for me?"

Her friend shook her head. "Write to me after he banishes you do the dark tower. I'm sure there's a footman so besotted with you he'd brave going against your father's wishes to deliver a letter to me."

Laughing, Phoebe sighed. "Well, then, I'd best get this over with."

She followed Marjorie into the entry hall, hugged her friend good-bye, then ascended the staircase to her father's office. The sounds coming from within the room told her he was opening and closing drawers, an odd habit he did when he was angry. She'd never been brave enough to ask what he looked for, and he always stopped when she came into the room.

"I'm here, Papa." She stopped in front of his desk to await his censure.

He slammed one more drawer shut, then straightened. His coat was unbuttoned, and he shoved it out of his way when planting his hands on his hips. Then he folded his arms across his broad chest, instead, still studying Phoebe. Finally, he swiped his palm over his balding scalp.

Shaking his head and lifting his arms in exasperation, he asked, "Am I to believe what I'm being told? You were taught better than that, so it can't be true. Were you at that man's house?"

Phoebe held his gaze with her head high. "Of course not, Father."

"I see you know of what I speak. Of course, you do. Is there any reason people will believe you were there?"

"I've done nothing I'm ashamed of, nothing that could hint something like this were true." She refused to beg him to believe her. Instead, she had to fight to keep her anger from her tight voice.

Father motioned to the chair beside her. "Sit." He sat in his own chair and arranged the items on the desk into military-straight lines and exact positions, a habit she'd also developed over the years.

When everything suited his preferences, he again met Phoebe's gaze. "Your mother told me you were receiving calls from Basingstoke and have been seen with him practically daily."

There was no "practically" about it, but she didn't say so.

"I didn't approve, but your mother convinced me it was for the better to allow it. She seemed to feel you might see the man behind our backs if I didn't." Papa lifted an accusing eyebrow. "This morning's newspaper has proven my original feelings were correct."

"I'm sorry to bring a hint of scandal on your name, Father, but the possibility of gossip exists no matter whom I'm seen with."

Father's piercing look held her. "Don't take me for a fool, daughter. Few men have as bad a reputation as Basingstoke."

"He hasn't done anything any number of men have also done before they marry."

"Phoebe, you cannot expect to justify his past actions by comparing them to others'. And you cannot be included in his future. End this now. Send him a note stating you wish for him not to call again. If not, I'll have your mother take you back to the estate, and I'll find a suitable husband for you. An impoverished vicar or widower with children should be willing to agree to marry you, if I make a large enough settlement on you."

I can't do that. Father can't do that!

She couldn't get the words out of her mouth. "Please..."

"If you've taken a foolish notion to marry the man, I'm sorry." Her father's terse expression softened. "Your mother should never have allowed you to know him well enough to form an attachment."

Her heart had attached itself to him long before this Season. By the time Mama had discovered Phoebe's inclinations, it was too late.

"I will leave the wording of your note to you, but I insist it be sent within the hour. We cannot wait a moment longer to stop this gossip and repair your reputation. Go, now, and get it done."

Several moments passed before Phoebe could stand and go to her room. She was being punished for something she hadn't done, and it would affect the rest of her life.

There must be a way to resolve this so she could still marry Basingstoke. She'd keep searching for an answer until she found it.

Chapter Six

It has come to my attention that the Earl of B~ hasn't been seen escorting Lady P.W.—

Phoebe scratched out the line in her journal, dipped her pen in the inkwell, and began again.

For weeks now, Lady P.W. and her wicked beau Lord B~ have been seen everywhere together. Balls, the theatre, the museum...anywhere a couple could be discovered.

Rereading her entry, she sighed and pushed away the book without blotting the ink. She could no longer pretend she and Basingstoke were together. As her parents had demanded, she'd written the earl, but it wasn't the polite note ending their new relationship. No, she'd scandalized her family once again, or would have if her letter was discovered.

Dear Lord Basingstoke, she began.

It is of the utmost importance I meet with you this afternoon. I shall be waiting at the three benches by the Serpentine at three o'clock.

Yrs., Lady Phoebe

She'd bribed the poor, sweet footman who was always eager to do her bidding, and he delivered the note post haste. She had no way of knowing if the earl received it right away, but she'd wait for him at the appropriate time. She had to hold strong to her belief she and Basingstoke were meant for each other, and that they'd find a way to survive this setback.

Twenty minutes before three o'clock, Phoebe found her mother reading in the morning room. "I'm going to call on Marjorie," she lied.

Mama turned a page without looking up. "Be home in time to dress for the musicale this evening. And give my best wishes to her mother."

"I will Mama." Donning her gloves and bonnet and summoning her maid, Phoebe hurried to leave before anyone could think of something to stop her.

A single woman walking alone in Hyde Park was unusual, but she tried to look hurried, as though she was catching up with her party. It was early for the fashionable crowd—she'd planned it that way to avoid drawing attention to themselves—so the paths were nearly empty.

As she rounded the bend in the serpent-shaped river, she saw a man standing at the shore near the benches, hands clasped behind his back. While he could be any tall, dark-haired man, her heart recognized him even from behind.

Basingstoke turned when she approached, and the sun shone off his teeth when he smiled.

Her stomach fluttered.

"Good day, Lady Phoebe."

"It's a very good day, sir." She hesitated in front of him, wanting something she couldn't name, then walked over and took a seat on one of the benches.

He followed her, but remained standing, kind enough to take the sun in his own eyes, not hers. "I was surprised to receive your note. Is something amiss?"

"No. Well, yes." The foolishness, the utter brazenness of her act struck her, keeping her from finding her words. "Did you read the newspaper this morning?"

"I did."

"Then you saw it."

"The gossip, yes."

She gnawed her lower lip, still struggling to make sense

of her tumbling thoughts.

"You want to know if it's true a woman left my home late last night."

"Oh, no, that's not it at all. It's none of my business what you—"

"Phoebe, no one came or left but me. I went to the club after we parted."

Her relief hit so deeply she almost didn't notice his use of her first name. When that fact sank in, her heart sang. "Believe me, that wasn't my concern. My father has me worried. He won't allow me to see you again."

"I see. To be honest, I'm surprised he allowed it to this point."

"Mama never said so, but I think she hoped that by getting to know you better, I'd see how poor a choice you were as a husband."

The corners of his lips twitched. "And have you come to your senses?"

She looked down at the tip of her boots, once again gnawing her lip. Then she peered up at him, bracing herself for humiliation. "No."

The lines around Basingstoke's mouth relaxed as his smile widened, lighting his face. "I'm pleased to hear that. What will you do?"

Why did he expect her to do something? He could resolve this issue by simply proposing. Father might refuse at first, but Mama could change his mind. Maybe. A proposal would make Basingstoke respectable, and let her parents see his intentions were honorable. Yet he didn't even hint at being close to asking for her hand in marriage.

Maybe he had no intention of doing so. She'd created his attraction in her dreams so long ago, and he felt nothing of the sort. He was being polite to a foolish girl, that was all.

She refused to allow that thought to linger.

What could she do to thwart Father's demands? She certainly couldn't call on the earl. And slipping out of the house on her own—as she'd done now—would make everyone think something illicit was taking place. There must be a way to see him.

The obvious answer was the easiest to accomplish. Tipping her head to one side, she grinned, quite pleased with herself. "Why, tonight I shall go to Lady Hasslebeck's musicale, and tomorrow, Miss Riverton's ball at Crighton house."

He nodded, his grin twitching as if he was fighting laughter. "I considered accepting an invitation to a Venetian breakfast that arrived this morning."

"What a coincidence. We received the same invitation."

She could see he understood. They could attend the same assemblies whether Father wanted her to or not, for as long as she remained in London. Basingstoke did want to see her again, to spend time with her. Those fears were for naught.

Mama would cluck her tongue disapprovingly when she saw him at so many assemblies they attended, and Father might follow through on his threat to send her back to the country, but she had to risk it.

She wished she could come right out and ask why he didn't propose. He must have some reason. Could she make some obvious hints to assure he knew she'd accept?

Oh, she was so foolish! Of course he waited. They'd met merely two weeks ago. No one should make such an important decision on such short acquaintance.

But her feelings wouldn't change no matter how long they knew each other. She would always love him.

"You'd better return home before someone recognizes you," he said softly.

"Yes, I should." She sighed. Someone needed to invite the two of them to a card party, so they could spend time together simply talking. Spend time showing Mama how well they suited, how happy they were. Surely that would make her mother realize the truth and convince Father this was best for Phoebe.

Lord Basingstoke was absolutely the best match for Phoebe.

Sitting in the dark corner of White's club the next afternoon, Basingstoke was brooding. There was no other word for it. Up until the last month, he could care less what Society thought of him. For the most part, he still did. The only opinions that mattered now were Lady Phoebe's and her parents. He supposed some sort of grand gesture was required to prove to them he wasn't the man he was reputed to be.

He didn't make gestures, grand or otherwise, to change anyone's opinion of him. Those who knew him recognized the man he was. Those who didn't...who cared?

Thornton found him in the shadows and sat in a chair close by. "What has you in such a grim state?"

"I'm not grim. I'm thinking."

"You look as if you're about to let go of one of your best land tenants. Whatever you're thinking of, stop."

"You're right. I shall stop. Why are you lurking in the shadows so early in the day?"

"Boredom. I have no excuse. I decided to find a game of cards winding down from last night and joining it in hopes of fleecing anyone with too little sleep and too much money still in his purse."

Shaking his head, Basingstoke chuckled. "You have more money than most of these men put together. Why even try to win more?"

Thornton shrugged. "Because I can."

Basingstoke pushed himself to his feet and stretched. "I need to clear my thoughts and you need to waste some money. Let's go to Tattersall's and examine the horse flesh. I'm sure they're selling off some stud or other worthy of your interest."

Rising, Thornton followed the earl. "That's a much better scheme than watching you contemplate whatever ills you've imagined."

The auction had already begun when they arrived, so there was little time to examine the items still to be bid on. Basingstoke squeezed through the crowd until he was close enough to see clearly what was on display.

Thornton found his way to Basingstoke's side, muttering, "The quality of people they allow in here..."

"I never knew you were a snob, Thorn. If a man has money, shouldn't he be allowed to spend it?"

"I never knew you were a champion for the common man."

Rather than responding, Basingstoke eyed the conveyance awaiting bids. A cabriolet in impeccable condition, it struck something inside him. Never one for ostentatiousness—his own vehicles were staid, black, and serviceable—this cabriolet was as attention-grabbing as any. The folding hood was black, yes, but the carriage body was a rich hunter green, and the spokes of the wheels were bright yellow. That punch of color made all the difference, and he knew Phoebe would love it.

Thornton must have had the same thought. "Your lady-love will look pretty when you take her for a drive in that."

Basingstoke's pride bristled, still wanting to appear aloof where his heart was concerned. "I thought only of myself. It's too bold for my tastes."

His friend simply eyed him, causing Basingstoke to grow uncomfortably warm.

"In that case," the duke said, "you won't mind if I bid."

"Of course not. Feel free to bid on anything that catches your eye. It's your purse we came to lighten, not mine."

"Excellent. That cabriolet will make an excellent wedding gift when a certain gentleman finally decides to propose."

"It's not a simple decision," Basingstoke said with a growl. "Marriage."

"The decision is already made. I can see it in your face when you look upon her. When you mention her name. When I mention it. Lady Phoebe Woodson. See, there, you did it again. Your brow goes soft, and your lips relax. She is a balm to your soul, man. Quit wasting your time."

Thornton was right—Lady Phoebe was a balm, but it didn't remove the obstacles in their path. "I knew I faced a difficult task, trying to find a respectable woman whose family wouldn't reject a disrespected man. I just didn't realize how much it would bother me when it came time to discuss the betrothal with her father."

"It doesn't help that you associate with *those* men." Thornton pointed to the *W* pin.

"Don't you start in on them. You haven't avoided the scandal columns, yourself."

"I'll hold my thoughts for now. Your cabriolet is next, and I don't want to distract you while you bid."

Basingstoke gave him a harsh glare but quit arguing the point and bid until the less-than-unassuming cabriolet was his.

Chapter Seven

All is well between Lord B~ and Lady P.W.
One expects to hear news of a betrothal soon!

Phoebe and her friends, Marjorie and Clara, paused in front of the haberdasher's shop and eyed the fabric displayed within. One of the bolts caught her eye. "Oh, my."

"Which one?" Marjorie asked. "The sprigged rose?"

"That red is divine!" Clara sighed. "I do wish red didn't make me look so sallow."

"That dark green would make a charming pelisse for you, though," Phoebe said.

Before she could suggest they go inside, Lord Basingstoke called to them from down the street.

"Lady Phoebe, ladies, it's a beautiful day for a stroll, isn't it?"

She spun to see him approach with the Duke of Thornton. "Your Grace, my lord, how good to see you. We were deciding whether or not to shop for fabric."

Basingstoke raised an eyebrow. "Don't let us keep you from such a delightful pastime."

Marjorie took a step away from the window. "We may shop anytime we wish." She nudged Phoebe's elbow.

"Yes," Lady Clara jumped in, clearly understanding Marjorie's ploy. "Anytime."

Phoebe took the hint. "We were about to continue on our way."

"Will you allow us to join you?" Lord Basingstoke approached, and Thornton followed.

"Delighted," Marjorie said. "Your Grace, I believe you and my husband were recently discussing a horse."

"Yes. Yes, we were." He passed Basingstoke to walk with Marjorie and Clara.

Phoebe watched them move away, then turned to Basingstoke and smiled. "I'm happy to see you."

"Happy doesn't fully express what I feel."

They walked slowly behind their friends with just enough distance that their conversation could be almost private. Phoebe toyed with the ribbons on her reticule, inexplicably nervous to be so near him again. "My friends and I needed a break from morning calls. I had no idea it would lead to seeing you. Are you also shopping?"

"I hadn't intended to, but while at Tattersall's I found a cabriolet I had to have. I paid a fair price for it. Luckily the other bidders realized how determined I was to have it, and they stopped bidding."

"How delightful." She didn't care one way or another about carriages and the lot. Men could carry on about them like...well, like she and her friends did over fashion, fabrics, and trims.

"I shall take you on a drive later in the week."

Even more delightful. But how was she to convince Mama to allow it? And keep Father from knowing about it?

He seemed to understand, or anticipate, her concern. "May I call on you at home a few times before then? Will your parents allow it?"

"I hope Mother's been taking to heart what I tell her about you, but she's not likely to stand up to Father's edict." Mama hadn't mentioned him that morning, which Phoebe preferred to think was an improvement. Likely nothing new had happened for her to complain about.

"You've been talking about me? All good, I hope." He

winked.

Phoebe's heart tumbled, stopped a moment, and then raced on. That wink was like a physical touch. She drew a deep breath and let it out slowly before speaking. "Is there anything else I might relate to her?"

"Not if you wish her to look kindly on me."

Now her heart stopped cold. What did he mean? Was there some new scandal marking his good name?

"I jest, dear girl," he said with a chuckle. "I didn't mean to alarm you. It was in rather poor taste, I'll admit. Forgive me. Look, we're lagging behind the others. We'd best catch up."

Thornton turned at the sound of their approaching footsteps. "Lady Phoebe, did he tell you of his purchase? I don't know what the man was thinking. Ghastly shade of green, and those wheels! Brighter than the sun, I tell you. So unlike him. One would think he was trying to please a lady—if one didn't know him better."

The cabriolet was for her? Or simply to delight her when they drove about? If she was ever allowed to be seen with him again. "It sounds charming."

With a brief nod, Thornton went back to speaking to the women on either side of him.

"It's not ghastly," Basingstoke said softly. "The green, that is."

"I never suspected it could be," Phoebe said. "I've seen nothing to dissuade me you have excellent taste."

His shoulders relaxed noticeably. "We're drawing near your home. I should leave you before anyone in your household spies us. I will see you this evening, as we discussed?"

"Of course."

He bowed, called to the duke, and the men turned at the corner. Phoebe and her friends continued on.

Clara watched the men walk away. "You are so lucky, Phoebe, to have secured the love of such a handsome man. Perhaps you could suggest his friend might wish to know me better?"

Marjorie laughed and shook her head. "As if anyone could convince Thornton what his own feelings are. You'd better set your sights elsewhere."

Phoebe held her tongue. No one could have imagined how she and Basingstoke came to fall in love, and look where they were now. It never hurt to dream.

It didn't hurt until Father objected, that is.

Then Basingstoke failed to attend the agreed-upon ball.

Chapter Eight

Mayhap the news of a betrothal between Lady P.W. and Lord B~ was spoken too soon. Has Lord B~ left town for the Season?

Basingstoke had as much as vanished from Society.

Over the course of the next three days and nights, Phoebe and her friends plotted and schemed over ways to find Basingstoke, to no avail. He didn't walk at the popular hour in Hyde Park. He wasn't in attendance at any of the five balls she attended. Yes, five balls in three nights. Each time Phoebe asked to leave one, Mama was livid at being pulled away from her friends just to return to the carriage and join the slow-moving traffic travelling four blocks to the next gathering.

Mama was slightly less distressed by Phoebe's insistence they accept invitations to two musicales and an afternoon of cards during that same period. As feared, Basingstoke was notably absent.

To get her away from her drastic imaginings, Marjorie insisted Phoebe join her friends for a visit to the Royal Menagerie at the Tower of London. "Lady Clara is among our group, and you've met the others."

"Very well," Phoebe had said, resigning to the fact she wouldn't see *him* yet again.

With three ladies and two gentlemen in their party, Phoebe didn't have to pay particular attention to either gentleman, to her great relief. She and Clara strolled ahead of the others once they passed through the gate.

Clara spoke to Phoebe in low tones to prevent the others from overhearing. "Marjorie says you haven't seen Basingstoke since I last spoke to you."

"No. I'm so frustrated. We'd been informing each other which assembly we planned to attend, so we'd see each other. Then he didn't come, and he hasn't been at any ball I've gone to. Mama won't allow me to flit from ball to ball of an evening any longer, so I must hold out hope he finds me."

"You assume he's looking for you."

Phoebe frowned at Clara. "Why would I wish to think anything else? The only answer I can find for Basingstoke's avoidance of me is Father must have spoken to him and scared him away."

"If he frightens that easily, his affection for you must be weak."

"I agree." Phoebe laughed at the ridiculous idea. In a tone of voice making clear her sarcasm, she added, "I must finally admit the truth and look elsewhere for a husband."

Clara laughed, tilting her face up to the sun, which made her red curls glow brightly. "You're going to be disappointed when you marry some other man. Who could compare to this image you've created in your head of Basingstoke?"

Who, indeed? No one could compare to the real man, much less the idealized one in her dreams.

They paused at a cage holding a golden jackal with a bright, silvery back. The creature was slim, sleek, and held its head low as it gazed at them, as uncertain of their purpose as Phoebe was of Basingstoke's.

"He looks ready to attack," commented Mr. Wilmot, who stood at her side.

A familiar voice spoke from beyond him. "And this, Benjamin, is Napoleon, small and fierce, and never to be trusted."

Basingstoke. How had he known she'd be there? He couldn't think they could steal some time alone at the menagerie. She laughed softly. What a silly notion, thinking he'd come there looking for her.

And where had he been for the last sennight?

Phoebe glanced at the jackal's sign, noting the name read *Billy*. Napoleon was a much more fitting name.

Curious as to the identity of this Benjamin to whom Basingstoke spoke, she leaned forward to peer around Mr. Wilmot. The only person standing with the earl was a young boy with the same thick, black, beautiful hair and strong brow. She gasped and straightened before Basingstoke caught her looking.

He was there with his son! Everyone knew about the boy, but in all the mentions of him, no one had mentioned actually seeing him. Reportedly, the child lived with his mother in a bawdy house near the club the earl frequented. It was disgraceful.

And until now, she'd thought it was all a lie. Her stomach felt queasy.

Firstly, no child should be raised in such a setting. A true gentleman would provide a proper home or foster the boy with a family in the country until he was old enough to be sent to school.

Secondly...well, she couldn't think of another reason to be outraged. She felt sorry for the boy, who seemed well-behaved and wasn't running madly, screaming like a banshee, as other boys were around them.

Realizing her friends were on their way to the next exhibit, Phoebe followed.

As did Basingstoke. "The eagle, Ben. Wellington is his name. He sees all and attacks when the time is right."

The sign said the bird's name was Tom. How undignified for such a beautiful creature. He deserved a proud name, something strong, like...well, like Wellington. Basingstoke was quite right.

As they moved on, he named the other animals. The

leopardess was Harriet Wilson, beauty that she was. Beau Brummel was the peacock roaming free, of course. The proud lioness lying some distance from her mate he called Countess Lieven.

But the last pair made her laugh out loud. A pair of hyenas, one noticeably rotund, he named, "Alvanley and his fat friend." Those were the words reported to have been spoken by Brummel, referring to the Prince Regent as the fat friend.

"Really, Basingstoke," barked Phoebe's companion Sir Phineas Taylor. "Have you no respect for your peers?"

Mr. Wilmot agreed and urged Phoebe to move on. "The nerve of the man bringing his bastard out among us like this."

Phoebe halted. How could Mr. Wilmot say such a thing within the boy's hearing? She glanced back at Basingstoke, who had his hand on his son's shoulder. A black cloud—that was the only way she could describe it, a black, threatening storm cloud—overtook his features. She was too embarrassed to say anything, and when he caught her looking, she turned away.

Ruffling the boy's hair, he said, "Come, Benjamin. I think it's time for an ice."

Smiling at his son as if nothing was amiss, he led him toward the exit gate.

Phoebe's heart went with him. No child should be treated that way, to be spoken about in such harsh terms within his hearing. Even if the child knew of his beginnings, to have it said out loud was intolerable.

Mr. Wilmot was no gentleman. As soon as she and her girlfriends were away from the men, she'd tell them she never wanted to endure the company of Wilmot and Sir Phineas again.

Chapter Nine

Has there been a falling out between Lord B~ and Lady P.W.? Lord B.~ hasn't graced the ballrooms of any of the recent assemblies. Has Lady P.W. come to her senses at last and decided upon a different young man?

Watching his much-younger brother enjoy a pineapple ice at Gunther's wasn't enough to put out the fire burning inside Basingstoke at Lady Phoebe's betrayal. She'd fooled him all this time. Made him believe she wasn't like the others where his brother was concerned. He'd only been away for a few days...was she angry at him for not telling her he was leaving? Or had her true feelings finally shown through?

The answer was clear. She hadn't chastised her companions when they spoke so cruelly about Ben. The boy wasn't the only child in London to be born outside marriage, nor was he the first not to be acknowledged by his father. Their father.

The late earl had died while Benjamin was still at his mother's breast, so at first Basingstoke had thought the lack of inclusion in his will was merely an oversight. Perhaps Father would have shown affection for his son.

Then he learned about the other children.

Their father wasn't an affectionate man. He'd never

spoken with pride about his elder son, never bragged about Basingstoke's accomplishments.

In his own childhood, Basingstoke hadn't noticed anything amiss in their relationship until he spent school holidays at the homes of his classmates. The laughter there, the obvious love, warmed him at the same time it made him feel alienated. He was an outsider, no matter how welcoming his schoolmates' families were.

He wanted something different for Benjamin. Born to his father's courtesan, Mrs. Minnie Smythe-Richards, the boy lived with his mother in a small, but clean, apartment next door to the house where she'd plied her trade. After his father's death, Basingstoke assured she had adequate income to support the two of them, so she needn't return to prostitution. He felt the time with a loving mother would give his brother a strong foundation upon which to build a life.

Now he was of age for schooling, so Basingstoke had moved Ben into his town home in preparation for living in the country under the tutelage of the man he'd just hired. He was not going to let their father's philandering scar his brother for life, and the first step involved distancing him from his mother. She'd complained at first, but an increase to her income had quieted her.

Five years ago, when Basingstoke had begun to call upon Benjamin, the rumors had started. No one knew of Ben's relationship to the late earl, so they naturally assumed he was Basingstoke's son.

Basingstoke wouldn't have been the first peer in his early twenties to have an illegitimate child, but that was just the sort of situation gossips sought to add to their repertoire.

And he didn't care.

His true friends knew him, and he'd always been sure that somewhere there was a woman who'd love him despite the scandal that wasn't even his own.

Seeing a dribble of raspberry ice about to drip on Ben's shirt, Basingstoke reached for his handkerchief. "You don't want to ruin that clean, white shirt."

"Mama never buys me ices," the boy said. "Are we going back to the mena-grie?"

"Is that what you want to do?" Enough of Basingstoke's anger had subsided, and he was reasonably certain Lady Phoebe and her friends would have left by now, so he felt safe in returning.

"Yes!"

"Well, then, let's be off."

When they arrived at the menagerie, he paid the admittance fee again and led Ben inside. "Where shall we begin?"

"The elephant!" The boy bounced with excitement and tugged on Basingstoke's arm. "Let's go!"

Chuckling, Basingstoke followed his little brother. "He's not going anywhere. He'll be there when we get there."

"But I want to *see* him. Come on." He added his other hand to the tugging and leaned back for more leverage.

"I'm coming."

No one stood near the elephant's enclosure, so they could watch without being rushed to move on. Birds hopped about on the stone floor, and one rode on the animal's hip. With his trunk swishing slowly side-to-side and his eyes closed, the elephant looked to be napping.

"He's sleeping. Isn't it time for you to do the same?" Basingstoke asked his little brother.

He received a glare in return. "I'm not a baby."

"Well, then, let's move on." He didn't pay much attention to which animals they saw. The sound of Ben's excited chatter was enough to prove how much fun he was having. Basingstoke also had fun but would have enjoyed himself more had he been able to spend the time with Lady Phoebe at his side.

The more fool he. Even as angry as he was at her inaction when her friends spoke ill about Ben, he couldn't put her out of his thoughts. Out of his plans for his future.

About half an hour later, he saw her standing with one of her friends in front of the eagle's cage. Checking about, he didn't see the rest of their party.

"Good afternoon, ladies. It's lovely weather, isn't it?"

Lady Phoebe spun around and smiled when she met his gaze, her eyes wide with surprise and what he hoped was happiness. "Quite lovely."

Her friend, whom he now recognized as Lady Clara Swinton, eyed him before giving Lady Phoebe a side glance. She said nothing.

"Your friends aren't with you?" he asked.

Lady Phoebe shook her head. "We weren't ready to leave when they were."

"Neither was Ben. He insisted we return." And Basingstoke was so glad he had. He winked at the beautiful woman in front of him. "Have they added any new exhibits while we were away?"

"I'm not sure. Shall we explore to find out?" Lady Phoebe glanced at Lady Clara, who nodded in spite of her eyebrows being drawn together in stern disapproval.

"Come, Ben," he said.

"I feel I must apologize for our companions earlier," Lady Phoebe said.

Unable to meet her gaze, he watched a mother and little girl peering at the leopards. "It's nothing I haven't heard."

"It was a disgusting thing to say. I'm embarrassed to call them friends."

"Phoebe," Lady Clara said, putting a hand on her arm, "let's not discuss them."

Lady Phoebe straightened her shoulders and held her head high. "You're right, they don't deserve our time. Benjamin, what's your favorite animal?"

"The lion. Rarrr!" He mouthed a huge roar and shook his head hard. "He's big, and strong, and no one wants to fight him."

"He is rather fierce, isn't he?" she agreed.

Watching her talk to the child warmed him. As he'd initially suspected, she didn't let the fact of his birth keep her from treating him as an equal. He lost himself in the pleasure he felt. "The lion isn't fierce. He has a severe case of biliousness and has no desire to hide his discomfort."

The ladies turned back and stared with wide eyes before breaking into laughter.

"Really, Lord Basingstoke, that's a bit much," Lady Clara chided as she fought to control her laughter. Her blue eyes sparkled.

"It's better than comparing them to the *ton*," Lady Phoebe said. "Well, more proper, I supposed, but not as funny."

Feeling quite pleased with himself, he tipped his hat. He was even more of a ninny than he'd realized, taking joy in her praise, weak though it was. "Well, then. You see Ben, we mustn't discuss our physical complaints, nor poke fun at Polite Society. I fear that leaves us with the weather."

Raising a hand to shade her eyes, Lady Phoebe looked skyward. "It's such a beautiful day, don't you think, Ben? Not a cloud in the sky."

"It's blue." The boy clearly had no interest in the weather. He peered up at Basingstoke. "Can we feed the monkeys, now? I'm bored."

Lady Phoebe quickly apologized. "We didn't mean to keep you from enjoying your afternoon. Please don't let us delay you."

Before she had the chance to leave, Basingstoke suggested, "We can talk while he feeds them. That is, if you ladies don't have somewhere else to be."

"No, we don't." Lady Clara replied.

"Excellent. We'll walk to the monkey cage together."

If Lady Phoebe didn't beat him to it, he'd drop a hint as to where he planned to be that evening, and tell her he was prepared to speak to her father as soon as he handled a few more matters.

Chapter Ten

I have the pleasure to announce a most delightful—but not unexpected—event to take place in the near future. It appears the banns will soon be read at St. George's for none other than Lady P.W. and Lord B~!

Two days later, when his butler announced Hartshorne's call, Basingstoke set aside the book he'd been reading and stood to greet the duke. "This is a surprise, Your Grace. Is something amiss with Lady Phoebe? Is she unwell?"

"She's the reason for my call, but her health isn't the issue. Read this." Hartshorne handed him a slim, leather-bound book.

"What's this?" He opened it and skimmed the first page.

The book appeared to be some sort of journal, and the first entry was dated three years ago. Each of the entries mentioned "Lord B~ and Lady P.W."

"Phoebe?"

The duke nodded.

"It can't be hers, however. We hadn't met three years ago, and I certainly wasn't courting her then." He flipped through to the ribbon marking the most recent entries. "According to this, I proposed last night."

"I'm assuming you didn't, because Lady Phoebe is at my

house as we speak, and she and my wife are calmly plying their needles and discussing some book or other. They'd be shopping for new clothing if a wedding was in the offing."

Basingstoke snapped the journal closed and set it on his desk. "How did you come by this? And should we be reading her private thoughts, fantasies though they are?"

"Do you have this morning's paper?" Hartshorne asked, ignoring the question.

Basingstoke picked up the folded newspaper and offered it to the duke, who didn't reach for it.

"Turn to Mrs. Crookshank's column."

He did. The third paragraph down was remarkably familiar. "Will banns be read at St. George's next Sunday for a certain couple we've been watching this Season? Anyone who saw Lord B~ and his lady last night would say so."

A proposal. It couldn't be. This was a coincidence. "She's Mrs. Crookshank?"

Hartshorne shrugged.

"No. I refuse to believe it." He picked up the journal and skimmed over the recent entries. "That column gossips about many people, not just me. There's nothing in this journal that doesn't include us, and no mention of anyone else that I see. I don't wish to intrude further on her privacy and read more."

"Perhaps she's one of many writers contributing to the column."

Tossing the paper aside. Basingstoke swallowed the bitter burn rising in his throat. Phoebe wasn't the sort of woman to do something so foolish, was she? That column had to be one of the main reasons her father objected to their friendship. "It can't be. Why? Why would she do it?"

"Why do women do anything? Maybe she created this dream after being jilted by some other man. Maybe she just has a vivid imagination. But on the chance she's only pretending to care for you, I felt you should read her journal."

Basingstoke glared at the unassuming book that appeared to prove he was being played the fool. He couldn't blame Phoebe without asking her the truth, but she'd likely deny it, regardless of whether she contributed to the gossip column or not. He handed the journal back to the duke. "You mustn't let her know you've shown me this. I'll discover the truth somehow. If she's guilty, at least I'll have found out before I do something foolish like proposing."

Once Hartshorne left, Basingstoke donned his hat and left his house. The only way to find out the truth was to call on the newspaper editor and grill him until he confessed.

Finding the editor bent over handwritten sheets of paper on his desk, Basingstoke tore into him. "Who is this Mrs. Crookshank of yours?"

"She is herself, of course, although it's a pseudonym. No one would allow her into their homes if they knew her true identity."

Could it be Phoebe? "How can you allow her to write these lies, day after day? One day you'll be threatened with libel."

The old man chuckled, adjusting his glasses with ink-stained fingers. "They threaten and threaten, but they have no legal case. No one is named directly, so if a man or lady wishes to believe the item is about him or her, so be it. Taking the matter to court would confirm their identity, which would only confirm the rumor to most of Polite Society, don't you think?"

Everyone knew who was being discussed, or accused, without an admission from the parties in question. They accepted it as fact. The editor's argument was weak, but true. Basingstoke decided to ask the writer's identity directly. "Is she Lady Phoebe Woodson?"

Raising his right eyebrow, the editor said slowly, "Oh, my. Would she be the Lady P.W. in this morning's paper? What did Mrs. Crookshank say about her? Ah, yes, a proposal. I must wish you well on your wedding, Lord Basingstoke."

"There is no wedding, which is why I demand to speak to Mrs. Crookshank. I have reason to believe it's Lady Phoebe writing at least a portion of that column. Tell me the truth!"

"I repeat: if the writer's identity were made known, she'd be ruined. You're wasting my time. Go ask your bride if she, herself, broke the news." In dismissal, the editor picked up another piece of paper and stared at it.

No one dismissed Basingstoke that directly and got away with it, but arguing was a waste of time, as the man said. He strode back outside and turned in the direction of Hartshorne's home. The time was now to get to the bottom of this situation. Did Phoebe love him, or was this all a game?

Turning the corner, he plowed into a woman. Grasping her arms to prevent her from falling, he looked down into a very familiar pair of eyes. Lady Phoebe's.

"Forgive me, my lord. I wasn't watching where I walked."

"Nor I." He studied her eyes in hopes of finding his answers there, then remembered where they were. "What are you doing in this part of the city? It's not safe for a young lady, even with your maid present."

The young maid looked away when he caught her watching him.

Lady Phoebe let her breath out in a huff. "I'm not a fragile porcelain piece. No one has accosted me."

"That doesn't mean it won't happen."

She was awfully comfortable walking in this neighborhood...as if she did it often. His stomach burned with realization. "You were on your way to the newspaper."

"How do you know that?"

She admitted it. The beginnings of a headache pushed against his skull. He couldn't admit how he knew without implicating Hartshorne. "Someone told me about the column. In fact, I just left the newspaper office."

"You spoke to Mr. Hillside, the editor?"

"I did." He shook his head. She knew the man's name. Basingstoke hadn't even asked when he'd barged in. Her guilt was all too plain.

"And what did he say about this morning's gossip?"

What did she expect the man to say? "Don't worry, he

didn't divulge the writer's true name."

She opened her mouth to speak again, but he interrupted her. "There's no purpose in giving him your latest *on-dit*. Come, I'll escort you home. That will stir many more tongues than your column would."

"What are you talking about? My column? I don't understand—"

"Don't waste your words on me." Walking briskly, Basingstoke took her directly home without saying another word.

Lady Phoebe remained silent, too, but he detected a quiet sniffle. He steeled himself against the sound, fighting not to succumb to her ploy for sympathy. He'd been so wrong about her, about who she was deep inside, and it was time to end the charade.

He stopped abruptly when they reached the corner where she lived. Drawing in a deep breath, he said, "You needn't fear I'll continue to court you. Your true feelings have been made clear and I won't bother you anymore. Good day." He performed a sharp bow and turned to walk the other way.

"Lord Basingstoke, I don't understand what I've done," she called after him. "Please explain—"

She was interrupted by her mother calling to her from inside the house. "Phoebe, come inside now!"

He didn't look back, but Phoebe said nothing more.

Basingstoke had too much business to attend to in Town to leave with Ben right away, but he could keep to himself and avoid anywhere he might cross paths with Phoebe. In time, his heart would heal enough to once again look for a wife. He dreaded the prospect, but in order for Ben and the others to receive the allowance that they deserved to receive for the rest of their lives, Basingstoke needed to ensure he had an heir. He couldn't trust his distant cousin to continue the payments.

No woman was going to stand in the way of ensuring Ben had a comfortable life, and the best chance at being accepted by society—those who mattered, at least. His brother deserved every advantage Basingstoke had, and he'd work as hard for that as if Ben were his own son.

Chapter Eleven

Did Cupid's bow miss? Lady P.W. and her earl were spotted arguing in the street. Rumor has it this might be the end of the journey for them.

Although Phoebe had hidden her journal in the bottom of her wardrobe the morning she and Basingstoke argued, never wanting even the slightest temptation to write in it ever again, she couldn't stop drafting her entries in her head. Nor could she quit reading Mrs. Crookshank's column. She was picking at the scab on her heart, certain that Basingstoke had already found someone else.

He'd been close to proposing to her. Her friends all agreed on that count. Then he blamed her for something she still didn't understand and disappeared from her life.

The hole he left behind could never be filled, no matter how many children she had some day with whatever man would have her as his wife.

This Season was now a waste of time and her father's money. The postulations of their argument and its obvious ending of any suit between them wouldn't fade from daily gossip until many months had passed. Why hadn't she listened to Marjorie and accepted the fact Basingstoke wasn't the man she should marry? She could have saved herself so much heartbreak.

But she wouldn't have experienced the joys of the time she spent with him. Even though she'd never be that happy again, she'd carry the memory in her heart. She now knew she was capable of loving as deeply as she had.

That happiness couldn't protect her from the stabbing pain that came when she read the latest entry in the gossip column. And her tears flowed heavily each time she did so. Rumors were being spread that Phoebe had once more been seen slipping away from Basingstoke's home late at night, more than a week since she'd seen him last.

Phoebe hadn't gone to a single ball since Basingstoke had berated her, so obviously she'd not been out that late. She didn't even know where he lived.

What a silly thought—she was making excuses for something she knew she didn't do. She was hopeless.

Had he found someone else, or was this someone he'd had a relationship with the entire time he was escorting Phoebe around Town?

Ben's mother. Yes, that must be who had been to his house. Now that Basingstoke allowed himself to be seen with the boy, he no longer needed to be discreet about his liaisons with the woman.

Shoving the paper aside, she drew up her knees and buried her face against them. That ever-threatening lump in her throat rose, and her eyes began to burn. Nothing would ever be right again.

A knock sounded on her bedroom door, and Mama called out, "Are you there?" She opened the door without waiting for a response.

Phoebe spoke into her damp skirt, not lifting her head. "As you see, I'm here."

"Darling girl, you need to come out of your bedchamber. You can't hide here forever."

"I only need to hide until the end of the Season." She hiccupped and sighed, trying to stop her tears. She was tired of crying.

Mama sat on the other end of the window seat. "I'll

tell your father we're leaving Town sooner than planned. We'll go home today. We don't even need to wait for all our belongings to be packed. We'll take only what we need for the trip."

As tempting, and as ideal, as the plan sounded, Phoebe couldn't bring herself to leave now. "I—I haven't found a husband yet. If we leave, Father will choose one for me, and you know the type of man he'll pick."

"You won't find a man while you're locked away in your bedchamber. We've discussed your chances here in Town. I don't think you'll care more for the men here who still seek a bride than one your father chooses. Let's go home."

Phoebe rolled to her feet, scrubbing her eyes with the butts of her palms. "I must speak to Marjorie."

Mama laughed as Phoebe stood. "You can't go anywhere looking as you do. Your eyes! Rubbing them so hard didn't improve their redness. I'll ring for fresh water to be brought up. A cold cloth will cool your face and reduce some of the swelling. Then your maid will restyle your hair, and you must wear a bright dress. Everyone is watching for a glimpse of you, so it's important you look like you aren't affected by the gossip."

All her mother's preparations were for naught, because Marjorie came to Phoebe before she'd even had her hair restyled, and was shown to her bedchamber.

Marjorie studied her face, likely recognizing the signs of her grief. "How are you? I haven't seen you since before...well, since *before*. I wanted to come sooner, but I feel so poorly in the mornings suddenly, and it doesn't improve much as the day passes."

"Are you unwell? You should be home resting."

Mama laughed softly. "Rest helps somewhat, but try having dry toast before you rise with some weak tea. Come, sit near the window so you can rest."

"My housekeeper also suggested dry toast. My mother had the same troubles early on."

"What trouble?" Phoebe asked, totally lost in the conversation. She glanced from one woman to the other. "If you aren't ill, what's wrong?"

The realization came slowly, brought on by the understanding looks her mother and best friend gave her. "Oh. Oh! When? When will you give birth?"

"Early in the new year," Marjorie said, her face glowing. "We're so happy."

Phoebe hugged her tightly. "You're so deserving, after all the two of you went through to finally marry. I can't wait to help you choose baby clothes, and bonnets. Do you think I could learn to knit booties?"

She and Marjorie studied each other in silence for a moment, then broke into laughter. "No, I suppose not. I've never been good at the accomplishments we were supposed to learn. I shall be the best aunt your children ever know, however."

"I'm glad for that, since I have no sisters or brothers."

"I'll come stay with you before your time and help you in the first few months."

Now Mama laughed. "You don't know the first thing about babies, dear."

"I know how to hold one," Phoebe insisted. "I can do so and allow Marjorie to sleep."

"And I shall appreciate you," Marjorie said.

Mama walked to the door of Phoebe's bedchamber. "I'll leave you two alone. Marjorie, you've already cured her melancholy, which is more than I hoped to see for some time to come. Thank you."

When she closed the door, Marjorie sighed. "Is it as bad as your mother makes it seem? Is there no hope for you and Basingstoke?"

"How can there be? I don't even know what sin he thinks I'm guilty of. I cannot defend myself, can't apologize. We are no longer speaking."

"Tell me again what happened. Your note was so brief..."

"Mrs. Crookshank's column said Basingstoke had proposed to me. I knew Father would be outraged that no one had spoken to him, and I was so upset this woman won't leave us alone. It's not fair that she tells such lies about people. She must know the effect her words have on our lives."

"Most people don't believe what they read there."

"Why do I hear the rumors repeated everywhere I go, then? I was so angry, I wasn't thinking clearly, so when I left your house I went straight to the newspaper."

"You should have had Hart go in your place, Phoebe. That's such a bad neighborhood."

"I told you I wasn't thinking clearly. I collided with Lord Basingstoke before I reached the newspaper office. He was so angry with me. His voice was sharp, his words terse. I don't know what I did to upset him."

"Think. What did he say?"

Phoebe searched her memory before speaking again. "He accused me of being on my way to the newspaper office, which I was. I don't know how he knew that, or why he was so angry when I confirmed it was so."

What had he said? "There was something about my *on-dits*, and not needing to give them to Mr. Hillside. What could he mean?"

Marjorie's eyes widened. "Oh dear. Oh, my. This is awful."

Phoebe waited impatiently for her to continue.

After an endless pause Marjorie did. "Do you remember my footman delivering your journal that afternoon you left it at my house? Hart found it, actually, and gave it to me."

"What does that have to do with Basingstoke?"

"What did you write in your journal that morning? You told me not long before you left in such a hurry."

Phoebe didn't see how her scribbles mattered. "I don't recall. Something silly about the earl and me. I haven't looked at my journal since that day."

"You said he proposed."

"I'm sure it wasn't the first time I said so. At various times I've had us married with a house filled with children, too."

"You wrote about the proposal. Mrs. Crookshank wrote

about an upcoming wedding. What if Hart read your journal...at least, that entry."

Phoebe shook her head. "I don't understand. Where does Lord Basingstoke fit into this story?"

Marjorie jumped to her feet and began to pace. "I'm only guessing. Was there even time for Hart to tell Basingstoke once he discovered the journal? He didn't give it to me until later that afternoon, and he made no mention of talking to anyone about it. I never would imagine he'd read something so personal."

Marjorie's speech began to race as her thoughts spewed forth, until she finally stopped. She offered Phoebe a pleading look. "All I can think is that Hart decided you are Mrs. Crookshank."

"Me? How utterly ridiculous."

"Men can be utterly ridiculous, you know. Some seem to do so more than others. Hart isn't one of those, but I cannot think of any other reason Basingstoke would have gone to speak to Mr. Hillside on the same day you did."

"How could he believe I could publish those awful things? About myself, no less."

"Phoebe, read your journal entries. If I didn't know the truth, I could easily believe it was gossip, not fantasies, on those pages."

Had she truly brought this on herself? "It can't be. Oh, what have I done? No wonder he refused to speak to me once he'd said his piece. What must he think of me?"

That awful swelling in her throat grew once more and began to burn. She'd destroyed her only chance at true happiness. She had no more tears to cry, so she couldn't release the pain inside.

There was only one way out of her pitiful mood. She needed a large distraction. "Tell me more about the baby. Have you chosen names? What color will you paint the nursery? Please, tell me all and save me from myself."

Phoebe was beyond saving, she knew, but somehow she must go on with her life. No matter how much it hurt.

Chapter Twelve

The Season seems so dull without reports on Lord B~ and Lady P.W...

Nothing could have surprised Basingstoke more than being told the Duchess of Hartshorne was calling upon him. "Show her to the drawing room," he told his butler.

He finished adding the expenditures in front of him before going to her. She stood stiffly looking out the window onto the street, her back to him. "Your Grace," he said, "how can I be of assistance?"

When she turned to face him, her expression was stern. "You will apologize to Lady Phoebe."

"I apologize?" What had Phoebe told her about their final conversation? "If I'd done something wrong, I would have done so immediately."

"You didn't let her explain her purpose that afternoon."

"I didn't need her explanation when it had been as much as confirmed by Hillside."

"Lord Basingstoke, will you truly take the word of a scandalmonger over that of the woman you love?"

He flinched. Everyone must know how deeply he and Phoebe felt about each other. He didn't want to imagine what the gossips claimed had torn them apart.

"My husband told you about Phoebe's journal, didn't

he?"

Dropping his gaze to the toes of his boots, he examined them as if he'd noticed a scuff. Then he cleared his throat. He and Hartshorne never should have read the book.

"I see he did. And the two of you concluded she wrote all those enticing tidbits in the paper that mentioned you." She shook her head and grunted in exasperation. "You men astound me sometimes!"

"If you assume the conclusion we reached, you've read her entries, too." Their thinking hadn't been far-fetched. "Why did her writings say much the same thing as Mrs. Crookshank's column on more than one occasion?"

She suddenly relaxed and took a seat. She shook her head once again and gazed out the window. "Phoebe has a creative imagination, and much of what she writes builds upon her daily life. But more of it is just the silly dreams most girls have of love and family."

"Those aren't silly dreams."

"They are when they involve a man one's parents would never approve of. A man with a sordid reputation who blatantly flaunts his disdain for Polite Society."

He wouldn't ask how long Phoebe had been pretending they were in love. He'd never forget his chagrin at learning they'd met some years ago and it hadn't stuck in his memory.

Phoebe would never forgive him for his treatment of her, but he couldn't live with himself without apologizing for his behavior.

As if reading his thoughts, the duchess rose regally and said, "I see I've made my point clear. I won't keep you. Good day, my lord."

Basingstoke watched her walk away. The woman carried herself as one expected of a duchess, yet she was so young. Phoebe was lucky to have such a good friend to help her recover from all the pain he'd caused. He must go to her and beg her forgiveness.

As to whether or not he would renew his attentions to her, that would require further thought. He had reason to believe there were two more children his father had never acknowledged, and Basingstoke couldn't quit searching for them now. Phoebe, or whichever woman he eventually chose to be his wife, deserved his full attention and he was too distracted currently.

Also, those searches led him to some horrid places in Town, the sort of places no gentleman would enter. He wished he still didn't care what people said about his being seen there, but whatever he did in his day-to-day life now reflected on Lady Phoebe.

While keeping their relationship at an end distanced her from the gossip, ever-so-slight as that distance was, he ached knowing the pain he caused her. But he had no choice, and he had no idea how long it might take to find those children. Let Phoebe believe he wouldn't eventually ask for her hand so she could go forward in her search for a husband.

She deserved to be happy, and he didn't have the right to stand in her way no matter how much he might come to love her.

Not even the news of Marjorie and Hart's pregnancy could carry Phoebe more than a day without Basingstoke entering her thoughts and dragging a heavy dose of pain with him. Mama repeatedly offered to return to their country home, but to do so would mean accepting the truth that her life would forever lack the love of her favorite earl.

When the house grew too warm to bear, Phoebe escaped to the pretty expanse of grass and flowers beside their home. The birds were quiet as if they also avoided the heat, but the roses and lavender shared their beauty with anyone passing by.

Stopping and snapping off a sprig of lavender, she inhaled its calming scent.

"I once offered you a rose, but it paled in comparison to these blooms. Do you tend them yourself?"

She spun around as soon as she recognized Basingstoke's voice. "I—yes, I do."

"Would it be redundant if I apologized for my lack of an apology for my recent behavior?"

Phoebe laughed, her eyebrows raised. She was too happy to see him to be angry. "I suppose it can't be redundant if you failed to do so the first time."

With his hands clasped behind his back, he smiled awkwardly. It was the first time Phoebe could recall him looking so uncomfortable. He didn't hold her gaze when he spoke. "I'm utterly ashamed of my behavior. You didn't deserve my accusations, nor my failure to allow you to defend yourself. You shouldn't have had to defend yourself. If I'd only asked you to explain the matter, I might have avoided causing you pain. But I was so angry." So hurt, he added silently.

"Marjorie guessed Hart had shown you my journal. I'm too embarrassed to even guess what you might have thought. I meant no harm, truly. And I never wrote for the newspaper."

Basingstoke took her hand and led her away from the street, rounding the corner of the house and stopping beside a section of the house that had no windows and was blocked from passersby by a tall hedgerow. "We shouldn't have read it. When Hartshorne offered it, I should have refused."

"I cannot blame you for making the conclusion that you did. I don't understand how Mrs. Crookshank's gossip so closely resembled mine on so many occasions."

"Can't you? She clearly understands what young ladies hope to experience, and what older ones find shocking. I feel responsible for opening you to such...such hurtful talk. It was never my intention."

What had his intentions been? At what point had he formed them? Phoebe was saddened to realize she'd never have the chance to ask him. Even if he desired her again,

Father would have none of it. Her dreams of marrying Basingstoke were done.

He squeezed her fingers. "Have I ruined any chance between us?"

"I'm sure we can remain friendly with one another."

"Is that all you wish for? Friends? Or do you tease me again? I've missed your sharp humor. Say you still care for me."

If she didn't care, he couldn't have wounded her so severely. No matter what happened in her life, she'd always have feelings for him. "I could never stop."

He smiled, and all the worry lines on his broad brow faded. "Nor could I. I was miserable without you. Before Marjorie convinced me of your innocence, I wished I had the ability to look past what I thought was a betrayal of our privacy. Force the anger aside and go forward with my plans for us."

"I'd never do that, speak of the private feelings between us. Well, to anyone other than Marjorie. Even Mama didn't know the whole of it."

"I know. I was foolish. Stupid. Completely blind to your true character." He pulled her closer, then lowered his mouth to hers.

The warmth of his breath on her cheek startled her almost as much as the feeling of his lips pressing against hers. Her stomach fluttered with excitement, and the skin on her shoulders burned where his hands rested. All too soon, it was over.

"Dare I ask if you'll marry me? I've wanted nothing else since I first met your gaze across the room at Almack's. I've grown to love you so, I can't imagine a future without you in it."

Laughter bubbled up from deep within her. "Yes, yes. Oh, yes."

With a wink, he said, "That's all you can say? Nothing of when you knew you loved me, or how the moments we're apart seem endless?"

"You are so arrogant." She did her best to look stern

but was unable to maintain the farce. "If you'd read my journal from the beginning, you'd know I thought I've loved you for years. It wasn't until I knew you better than I discovered what love really is."

Basingstoke raised her hand to his lips and pressed a kiss there. "I hope your love grows the more you know me. I know mine will increase with every moment we're together."

Phoebe was too lost in his gaze to put words in a sensible order.

"I must speak to your father," he continued. "Dare I hope he'll approve of our marrying? Or must we wait until you're of age to wed?"

"I'll ask Mama to be there with you. She'll convince Papa we must be together."

"Let's go to it, then. I can't wait a moment longer to tell the world Lady Phoebe Woodson loves me."

She couldn't say for certain her feet touched the ground as they walked to the house. She was so lighthearted she doubted she'd ever again soil her shoes. Lord Basingstoke loved her.

Chapter Thirteen

It has happened. Lord B~ has proposed to Lady P.W. and she has accepted.

Walking beside Phoebe toward the door to the house, realization broke through the elation overflowing in Basingstoke's thoughts. He slammed the butt of his palm against his forehead. "Blast it!"

He spun away from her. This wasn't how he'd planned his call. He was to have apologized and let her go on with her life. Instead, she was now waiting for him to speak to her father.

"My lord? Are you unwell?"

"Yes. No! That is, I—"

When he said nothing more, Phoebe spoke softly. "It's all right, you know. If you don't wish to marry me, that is."

How could he be such an imbecile? He faced her, tucked her hand into the bend of his arm and led her back into the garden. "I've made such a mess of things."

She said nothing.

"Where do I begin? You met Benjamin. Well, I neglected to introduce him. Ben is my brother." He let that statement hang for a few moments before going on. "I have three brothers and a sister...that I know of so far. I believe there are two more I haven't yet uncovered."

"They are...your half-siblings?" she asked when he met

her gaze.

"Yes. Not my bas— They're my *father's* natural children."

"I see. And you've never clarified to anyone that Ben isn't your son."

Basingstoke scowled. "Why should I? I acknowledge him as my brother anywhere that matters, which is not in Polite Society. They don't deserve to know him."

He paused and turned to face her. "My father never acknowledged any of the children, but he'd been paying Ben's mother for his needs. When Father died and the money stopped, she came demanding more money."

"And you paid, of course," Phoebe said.

He nodded. "I went further, setting up an allowance through my man of business. Then another woman came to me. She'd been a maid at our house here in town until father got her with child. He sent her away with no references, no money. I sent her to Basingstoke Manor, gave her a job, and set up an allowance for her daughter."

Basingstoke went on to detail the other children, the conditions they lived in with no help from the former earl. Acid burned inside him, leaving a sour taste in his mouth, but he forced himself to leave out no facts.

"When you found these women, your siblings...those were some of the stories that were told about you, weren't they? The houses of, er, entertainment." Her face was pink but she held his gaze.

"Yes. I fear I'm rather a dull man. I'm blamed for the sins of my father."

She smiled softly. "Never let that be known. I can't allow Polite Society to believe I fell in love with a dullard."

"There's more I must say, and it won't make either of us happy. I do wish to marry you, but I can't stop looking for those other two children."

"I would never ask that of you. Of course, you must find them."

"I'm afraid I can't marry you until I do."

Phoebe's brows drew together, a deep crease marring

the smooth skin between them. "I don't understand."

"The gossip will continue while I call on those neighborhoods, and your name will be dragged into the scandal."

"It's not a scandal if they're mistaken about what you're doing, Basingstoke. Even my parents will understand that."

"I hate thinking your good name is being ruined because of me," he said.

"I hate that those horrid people are lying about you. But I can't stop them, and neither can you. Let me be there beside you as you locate the last of your brothers and sisters. I'm proud to love a man who takes care of his family like this."

Basingstoke studied her for a good, long while. It could take years to know for certain he'd found all the children. Years during which he and Phoebe could be having children of their own. Their children would be victims of the rumors, too.

"Why have you kept their relationship to you a secret?" Phoebe asked. "You're willing to be seen with Ben in Town, but you haven't formally said he's your brother. Wouldn't doing so remove the fodder for gossip?"

He shook his head. "They'd still talk."

"You stubborn man. Yes, they'll gossip, it's what they do. But they'd leave your name out of it, and your reputation wouldn't suffer."

"My reputation has only been a concern where it reflects on you," he said honestly.

"Then change it. Why, if I let word spread about how you're helping your siblings, your reputation would soar. Please, give me permission to do so."

He didn't like being spoken about, period.

"My father would be proud of you."

That struck him in his heart. His own father had never shown pride in anything he'd done, not excelling in school or mastering any given sport he put his mind to. Had he really been mucking up his own path to happiness all this time?

She must have seen the tension leave his face. "Will you talk to Papa now?"

From above came the sound of a window opening, followed by her mother calling, "Phoebe, is that you?"

Without looking away from Basingstoke, she called back, "I'm coming inside now, Mama."

She turned toward the house but waited for him to join her.

Basingstoke had never spent time imagining how he'd feel knowing he was to ask for permission to marry a man's daughter, but he never would have dreamed he'd feel this ill. The rest of his life lay in the hands of the man he was about to face.

He'd never felt so powerless.

The sensation of powerlessness continued when he was shown into Lord Appledown's library, where Phoebe's father sat behind a desk that was smaller than Basingstoke would have imagined a man of his stature, both in build and in rank, would possess. Stopping in front of the desk, he nodded in acknowledgement. "Thank you for seeing me, sir."

Appledown set down his pen and leaned back in his chair, studying Basingstoke's features. "In truth, I've wondered if this day would come. My wife kept me apprised of your seeming pursuit, then dodge, of my daughter, but I hadn't heard of this most recent turn. I assume that's what you're here for. To ask for her hand?"

"Yes, sir. I—"

"Are you certain this time?" Phoebe's father interrupted. "I'm leery of giving her to a man who doesn't know his own feelings."

"My feelings for Lady Phoebe have never been in doubt." Well, other than when he was certain she was Lady Crookshank, but he wouldn't share that with her father.

"So you say. But what a man does means more than what a man says."

"I agree—"

"Then I suggest a long engagement so my daughter can see you are certain you care for her."

Frustration and indignation bubbled up and Basingstoke refused to be interrupted until he spoke his piece. "Lord Appledown, I am fully aware that Lady Phoebe has borne the brunt of much gossip where I'm concerned. And, that is not likely to change for some time. My father wasn't a good man. I'm not sure if you're aware of it, but he fathered many children after me, none of whom were my mother's issue."

He drew in a quick breath. "I am not my father. Nothing matters more to me than my family, those whom I love more than anything. As long as it takes, I will search for my siblings and see that they are given the chances due the children of an earl."

Basingstoke was surprised Appledown hadn't interrupted, but he continued without giving him the chance. "This search will take me into unsavory parts of town, and we've already seen what the gossips will make of my being seen there. Again, this will reflect on my wife. My original intention was to wait until I'd found them all before marrying."

Now Appledown began to speak, but Basingstoke cut him off.

"I cannot do so. I cannot give such power over my life, my happiness, to a Society which matters little to me. I can't miss out on the years of joy, of happiness, I can share with Phoebe. The years of love she deserves. I agree to a sensible period of engagement, but no longer than that."

Appledown waited a bit, his reaction kept hidden, then he leaned forward and rested his elbows on his desktop. "I see you do know your own mind. That pleases me. I don't need to ask if you've spoken to my daughter about this, you wouldn't be here if you were uncertain of her feelings. We can have the bans read at St. George's soon, or marry from my estate or your own. I leave it up to you."

Basingstoke let out the breath he'd been holding unaware. "Thank you, sir. I'll let Phoebe and Lady Appledown make those decisions, just as long as we are married before, say, the end of the year."

"Yes, well, go along then." Appledown reached for his pen with one hand and waved Basingstoke away with the other.

Leaving the library with a much lighter step, Basingstoke almost collided with Phoebe as he turned in the hallway. He caught her shoulders and they both laughed nervously. "He gave his approval."

She nodded, her face glowing bright with emotion. "I heard."

"Then you also heard the rest of what I said?" he asked quietly.

"I admit to listening beside the door. I wanted to be ready to step in if he refused you."

Basingstoke lowered his brow in a mock frown. "You doubted my ability to state my case effectively?"

"No, not really. And I'm so glad I listened. Do you really mean what you said?"

"About you? About family? Yes. I thought I'd said as much to you in the garden."

"Hearing it said so adamantly to my father gave so much more passion to the feelings. I'm so lucky, so honored to love you."

Knowing full well her father sat just inside the room, all Basingstoke could do is take her hands in his and kiss each one. "Not nearly as lucky as I am."

Chapter Fourteen

As rumor has it, love is very complicated for Lord B~.

Two days later, as Phoebe sat in the morning room reading the newspaper, Mama peered over her shoulder. "Daughter, you aren't reading that gossip column again, are you? Will you never learn?"

"I now know for certain there's no truth in anything written here, so where's the harm?" This morning, several of the names—or initials, since names weren't mentioned—were unfamiliar, which reduced some of the fun. Then she saw mention of Lord B~.

Lord B~'s inamorata, and mother of his child, is well known to be Mrs. M. S-R. What hasn't been told is that Mrs. S-R. is the cousin of Lady P.W., whom he's set to marry.

Phoebe shoved the paper aside. "Now they've gone too far. They claim Ben's mother is not only Basingstoke's lover, but she's my cousin. If that were true, you would have told me that night he first asked me to dance."

"You see?" Mama said. "You must stop reading that

column. Any column of the sort. Now you have even more distress."

"I don't have a cousin with the initials S-W., so the point is moot. Isn't it?" When Mama didn't respond, Phoebe turned to face her.

Mama crossed the room and sat in her favorite chair, picked up her needlepoint, and set it on her lap. She didn't take up the needle, but instead simply smoothed the canvas. At last, she spoke. "Smythe-Richards is the name she began to use after Ben was born."

Merciful heavens, it was true. Basingstoke and her cousin were lovers. A bit of gossip that had appeared several times came to mind. "You never thought I should know? Does she look like me? But wait, she was his father's lover. But does she look like me?"

Frowning, Mama studied Phoebe. "I suppose so. Her coloring is similar, as is her height. Why do you ask?"

"She was seen leaving his home late at night."

"That's odd. Are you certain?"

"Mrs. Crookshank suggested I was seen, but since I know I have never been to that house, she must have gone to him there, instead of wherever they usually met."

Mama shook her head. "That can't be right. You're mixing up the facts. Minnie's relationship was with the late earl. Your Basingstoke's father."

"Apparently my earl fell for her charms as well. He must have. She was seen."

As the idea of that sank in, the other side of this news became glaringly obvious. "You never mentioned I had a cousin Minnie."

Mama sighed and looked toward the window. "We could hardly admit to her."

"She couldn't have been a courtesan her entire life. Why did you say nothing while I was growing up? Why haven't I met her?"

"Her mother was kept by a viscount who won't be named. There's nothing to be gained from knowing his name. That man was Minnie's father. So you see, we couldn't speak of Minnie or her mother."

Phoebe let that news sink in. There were so many new balls to juggle, she had no idea how to juggle them all. Basingstoke's illegitimate brother. Phoebe's illegitimate cousin. How many more skeletons lurked in the closets of the two families?

Another realization dawned on her. "Benjamin is my cousin."

"Yes, dear. I understand he's a delightful boy."

"He is. You've never met him?"

"I couldn't draw attention to my connection to the child without tainting your name. I was protecting you."

That's what mothers did, Phoebe understood. They shielded their children from any and all potential threat to their well-being. Fathers did so, too, and older brothers. Basingstoke clearly loved Ben and he was willing to brave the gossip that came from taking his brother out in public.

"Still, Mama, at some point in recent months I deserved to know where I fit into this—this farce." She didn't expect a response, but she felt better for having said so. The frustration of the entire situation made her clench her fists.

What a match they were, she and Basingstoke. Innocent victims to scandal brought on by family. She thought she knew him so well, but clearly, she didn't. Oh, she knew his character, the essence of him that told her what he would or wouldn't do...at least, when she trusted herself to believe it. But their pasts, their histories, were something they needed to discuss, if nothing more than to prevent misunderstandings such as this.

Misunderstandings that would cause either of them to doubt the other. Life held too many pitfalls as it was; adding the potential for more was ridiculous to the extreme.

"Mama, may I send for Basingstoke? I need to talk to him."

"Of course. Write your note and one of the footmen can deliver it."

"Thank you." Phoebe went upstairs to write to him,

trying to formulate her message as she climbed the steps. There was so much to say, so many versions of "I'm sorry" to impart. Even if she spent a lifetime apologizing, she could never atone for the ugliness she'd thought Basingstoke was capable of. He deserved so much better than her. All she could do was to strive to be the kind of wife he deserved.

When Basingstoke received Phoebe's note asking him to call, he assumed she had more wedding details to discuss. He never imagined there were so many decisions to be made. What he truly didn't understand is why they couldn't be made without his input. Men took care of obtaining the license, securing the preferred time at the church, and all the financial dealings with the bride's father. They didn't care about anything more.

Yet he couldn't tell Phoebe that.

After being shown into the drawing room of her father's house, Basingstoke watched the traffic pass by the window while he waited.

Phoebe came in, but her expression was unreadable. Where was the overflowing joy she should feel?

"You look well, my dear," he said. "Have I told you today how much I love you?"

Her cheeks pinkened and she glanced at the open door. "I love you, too. And I must apologize once more."

"Relieve yourself on that thought. We've said all that's needed. Our misunderstandings are in the past."

"*Now* they are, yes. Mama told me about Minnie, and I must know something. It won't change how I feel about you, but I can't put it out of my thoughts until I know. Is Minnie the one who was seen leaving your home several times?"

That's what concerned her? After all they'd been through, she still didn't trust him? The thought sliced deep inside him. "I've never had that woman in my home. During one of the times Crookshank mentioned it, I was in the country making arrangements for Ben to move there. Another time I told you I was at my club."

A thought occurred to him. "I brought Ben to my home to stay until I can take him to the country. Maybe Minnie visited him on those nights she was seen."

Phoebe's face brightened. "Ben will live with you? With us?"

"Nearby. I purchased a cottage for Ben and a tutor, and will enroll him in Harrow when he's of age."

"You are such a loving man." She walked to him and wrapped her arms around his neck. "Such a good man. I'm so lucky to have your love."

"I'm the lucky one, Phoebe. I don't know what I've done to deserve your affections, but I will strive to be worthy of it the rest of my days."

She rested her head on his shoulder. "I do wish you'd trusted me with knowing Ben is your brother, not your son."

"Would it have changed anything between us?"

"No. It might have relieved some of my... Hmm. No, that's not right. My anxieties are my own to relieve, they're not your responsibility. But can you understand how confusing it was to learn Ben was your brother, despite what the gossips claim? I never heard a hint you shared a father. And then to discover Minnie is my cousin—"

Grasping her shoulders, Basingstoke pushed her back so he could look into her eyes. "Your cousin?"

"You didn't know, either?"

"I know nothing more about her than she was my father's mistress. I never cared to learn more. It was due to her station, you understand. I had nothing against her personally. She's a kind person and a loving mother."

"Our lives are permanently tangled together, even before we marry."

Basingstoke noticed a gleam in her eye and feared there might be more. "There's nothing else I should know, is there? I can't imagine any more long-lost relatives reappearing to cause us stress."

"If anyone else attempts to come between us, they'll face a battle they can't imagine. Nothing will stop me from loving you. Forever."

"Forever. Such a lovely word. I shall have it engraved on the inside of your wedding band."

She smiled and held him tightly.

He returned the hug. Forever. It was such an intangible word, until one spoke of love. Never-ending, eternal, lasting long beyond the end of their lives. "Forever. Yes, I shall love you until then."

Thoughts of wedding plans hovered in the back of his mind, but he no longer dreaded helping make decisions. These were the first of many to be decided upon by them both. He was a lucky man to be allowed such tasks with Phoebe.

Yes, he was besotted. Yes, he was a ninny, but he'd never admit it to his friends. But if this was what it was to love, he welcomed the weakness. Phoebe was the most important thing in his life, and he'd spend the rest of his days thanking her for allowing him to love her.

Love. Forever. Always. Three words that were so alien to him just months ago, and now they were a permanent, important, part of his vocabulary. As was one other word. "Wife. That was always such a serviceable word to me, a necessary position to fill in the course of fulfilling my duties to the earldom."

"That's what I am? An employee?" She didn't pull away, and her voice held restrained laughter.

"No, nothing like it. I was reflecting on how words become clearer when they're experienced rather than spoken."

"I see. Like husband. And one day, baby."

His heart swelled so much he thought it might explode. "Yes. Family, too. For the first time, these words are so beautiful. And I get to share them with you."

Basingstoke couldn't be any more blessed. And it was all

due to a beautiful minx who locked her hazel eyes on him across a ballroom and never let him go. He tightened his arms around her once again. “I shall never let you go.”

Epilogue

Lord B~ has been seen about Town absent a prominent piece of jewelry. Has he finally given up his wicked ways?

Uncertain who would be at The Wicked Earls' Club this early in the day, Basingstoke entered and checked the rooms. Most were empty, but the Earl of Woodcliffe sat reading the newspaper in one of the smaller sitting rooms.

He looked up and nodded his greeting.

"You're here early," Basingstoke commented.

"As are you." Woodcliffe grinned.

"I have much to do today and need to get this out of the way." He pulled the *W* pin from his pocket. "It's time to retire this."

"I heard the news. Congratulations on your upcoming nuptials."

Basingstoke nodded. "We're running out of members as each one marries and no one is brought in to replace them. Are you afraid that replacing us will lead directly to your own wedding?"

"Don't mention that word around me. I'm hearing it all too often as it is."

Tossing the pin onto a nearby table, Basingstoke chuckled. "The act of proposing is actually quite painless. It's the work involved in reaching that point that is such a nuisance. I'm handing the baton off to you. Carry it well."

With a wink, Basingstoke left the club. His solicitor had papers for him to sign, and then he was due to pick up Lady Phoebe at the modiste so they might drive in Hyde Park with all those people who didn't matter.

Yet Phoebe wanted to be seen with him, and what Phoebe wanted, he would provide. In two weeks, they would marry, then escape Town and begin their life together out of the eye of so-called Polite Society. Never again did he wish to hear the word wicked attached to his name, nor that of his brothers.

He was Basingstoke, and he carried the title proudly despite the damage his father had brought to it. Nothing anyone called him could change who he was, and he owed it to Phoebe to have taught him that.

Phoebe. Soon to be his bride, his wife, the mother of his children.

His love.

****I hope you enjoyed Basingstoke and Phoebe's story. Keep reading for a sample of Earl of Woodcliffe.****

Excerpt: Earl of Woodcliffe

April 1817, London

The burning sensation in William, Earl of Woodcliffe's, gut had nothing to do with the amount of liquor he'd imbibed the night before. It wasn't the result of eating too many petit fours in Lady Billingfield's card room. No, the sole reason for his distress was the size of the vowels he'd been forced to render to the Marquess of Markham in said card room.

With his pockets to let, he had no means to pay even a portion of the sum, and Markham expected payment in full today. Woodcliffe couldn't ask his best friend Jonas Tatum for a loan—he owed the man too much already. No, the only thing to be done was approach Father once again and admit how he'd lost all his money.

He rode to Mayfair shortly after rising before he could come to his senses and leave Town. Simpson, Father's butler, greeted him as he entered the house. "My lord, you're here early today."

"Too early for my tastes. Is Father in his office?"

"Yes, sir. Shall I tell him you're here?"

"No. Better I surprise him so he can't turn me away." Drawing a confidence-building breath, Woodcliffe strode upstairs and down the hallway, pausing just before reaching the door to his father's office. There was still time to turn around. He could go home to Middlecroft and hide until he had some funds.

If only he believed Markham would let him off that easily.

The double doors were open, and the sweet fragrance of Father's pipe tobacco filled the air as he entered. The massive desk and dark wainscoting added an austere look to the dark room with its deep green paint and tall bookcases. It suited the man, the second Duke of Cainbridge. He took himself quite seriously, rarely smiled, and expected more from his son than Woodcliffe could ever supply. Love was there, he supposed, but it wasn't demonstrated and never spoken of.

"Good morning," Woodcliffe said with all the cheeriness he could muster.

Glancing up from his newspaper, Father wordlessly lifted a fuzzy, black caterpillar eyebrow.

"I was out for a ride and thought I'd say hello."

"Don't give me that falderal. If you're here for breakfast, have Simpson order a plate from the kitchen." He lifted the paper, screening his son from his view.

"No, thank you. I ate at the club." He hadn't gone anywhere near the club in fear Markham would still be playing cards and would insist on payment of Woodcliffe's debt, but he hoped the idea of a proper meal made him appear more of a capable adult, which he was. Anyone could have landed in his position. Anyone except Father, that is.

"Get on with it, then. Why are you really here?"

"I've come for an advance on my allowance."

"You have. Well then." Neatly folding his newspaper and setting it aside, Father pulled out a drawer and withdrew a slim black leather binder. Opening it on the desk, he thumbed through the pages filled with his scrawled columns. "Ah, here we are. Let's see...yes...carry the five...Well, adding up your prior advances, you've spent your income until you're forty-three."

Woodcliffe coughed, lowering his gaze. Surely, he hadn't

asked for as much as that. "My need is rather urgent. If you could give me even half of my quarterly, it would suffice."

"What do you need it for this time? Damages from a brawl? Behind on your rent? Or have you lost another wager?" His father's scowl made Woodcliffe flinch. "This is the very reason I haven't turned over the management of the money to you. I fear what a mess you'll make of things when I'm gone. Everything I've acquired, everything not entailed, will be thrown away within months, I have no doubt."

"Cards, sir. I was certain my luck was turning if I just played one more hand."

Drumming his fingers on the polished wood of his desk, Father studied him for a bit before asking, "And how many more hands did you play after your money ran out?"

"I lost count after ten."

Father leaned back in his chair, rested his elbows on the arms, and steepled his fingers. "I'm not going to ask who you owe this time. It doesn't matter. I'm not rescuing you."

Woodcliffe's eyes widened, and he broke into a cold sweat. "But sir—"

"You're thirty years old—"

"Twenty-nine," Woodcliffe inserted.

"And it's time you took some responsibility. Pay your own debts. Settle down and find a nice, respectable young lady to marry. Not too rich, or you'll drain her accounts, too. Grow up, my boy, it's past time."

"But..." He couldn't come up with a reasonable excuse to delay the inevitable. One day he'd marry, just not today...or this year. Father was wrong about one thing, though. He was too proud to spend his wife's money.

Try as he might, he was unable to admit what had actually happened to his money. Yes, when he was in his early twenties, he'd had a bad gambling habit. Since he only played cards at the private club he and his friends belonged to, the losses had been easy to control. He won as often as he lost, and only toward the end of a quarter did his allowance run dry.

By the time he was twenty-five, he'd learned to read his opponents better and took his gambling to other tables, clubs, and private card games. It didn't matter. He was good, and he made money. A goodly sum, most of which he placed in a private account in a different bank than his father used, so his father had no control over the funds. No one could access them except Woodcliffe and his secretary, Eli Grainger.

Yes, Woodcliffe was excellent at reading a man's expression at the card table. But he was deplorably naïve when it came to knowing whom he could trust. And he should never have trusted his secretary.

Common sense told him that when he found Grainger, the money would be gone, but he was determined to find the man and see that he was duly punished. In the meantime, there were bills due and a need for trivial items such as food. As he'd expected, his father wasn't going to help him. He rose without comment.

Woodcliffe left as gracefully as he could, tossed a coin to the boy holding the reins of his horse on the street, and trotted off with no destination in mind. There must be a way to borrow money from someone. Who hadn't he borrowed from lately, and which among those men did he not already owe money to? If he couldn't think of anyone, he'd find some poor fool to play cards with and win enough to appease Markham for a time. Markham was not a patient man.

About the Author

USA Today Bestselling Author Aileen Fish is an avid quilter and auto racing fan who finds there aren't enough hours in a day/week/lifetime to stay up with her "to-do" list. There is always another quilt or story begging to steal away attention from the others. When she has a spare moment, she enjoys spending time with her two daughters and their families.

She also writes steamy romance under the pen name Ari Thatcher.

http://aileenfish.com
Facebook
Twitter

Made in United States
Troutdale, OR
03/31/2025